GIRLS RULE!

■ ■ ■ ■ ■ ■

GIRLS
RULE!

Phyllis Reynolds Naylor

DELACORTE PRESS

Published by
Delacorte Press
an imprint of
Random House Children's Books
a division of Random House, Inc.
New York

Visit us on the Web! www.randomhouse.com/kids
Educators and librarians, for a variety of teaching tools, visit us at
www.randomhouse.com/teachers

Library of Congress Cataloging-in-Publication Data
Naylor, Phyllis Reynolds.
Girls rule! / Phyllis Reynolds Naylor.
p. cm.
Summary: The Malloy girls and the Hatford boys try to outdo each other in a
quest to earn money and choose how to participate in the annual Buckman,
West Virginia, Strawberry Festival.
ISBN 0-385-73139-6 (trade) — ISBN 0-385-90170-4 (GLB)
[1. Sisters—Fiction. 2. Brothers—Fiction. 3. Moneymaking projects—Fiction.
4. Neighbors—Fiction.] I. Title. PZ7.N24G1 2004 [Fic]—dc22
2003016241

The text of this book is set in 12-point Adobe Garamond.

Book design by Trish Parcell Watts

Printed in the United States of America

September 2004

10 9 8 7 6 5 4 3 2 1

BVG

To Kristin Corcoran

Contents

■　■　■　■　■　■

GIRLS RULE!

■ ■ ■ ■ ■ ■

■ ■ ■ ■ ■ ■ ■ ■ ■ ■ ■

One

■

The Trouble with Being Nice

Caroline Malloy decided to be nice. If she was ever going to get all the things she wanted in this world— all the things she *deserved*—she would have to start thinking of others first.

She knew she had been selfish too often since her family had moved to Buckman. Now she was ready to show the people of West Virginia just how sweet she could be. *Because*—Caroline had found out that there was a strawberry festival in Buckman every June. In every festival there was a parade. In every parade there was a queen—the Strawberry Queen of Buckman.

Caroline was beautiful, wasn't she? She was talented and she lived in Buckman. So if she put her mind to it, why shouldn't *she* be queen of the Strawberry Festival?

"Because," said her sister Eddie, the oldest of the Malloy daughters, "you have to be a woman, not a girl, to be queen."

"A *college* woman," said Beth, the middle sister.

"And you have to be *chosen,* you can't just volunteer," said Eddie.

For a while Caroline was down in the dumps, but then she thought about something else. Didn't queens have ladies-in-waiting? There had to be helpers, didn't there? And wouldn't they ride on the float along with the queen? How did they get to be helpers unless they were chosen? *That* was when Caroline Malloy, precocious fourth grader, decided to be so nice that people would hardly recognize her, beginning at home.

"Do you want me to set the table, Mother?" Caroline asked that evening before dinner.

Mrs. Malloy turned and stared at Caroline. "Why, I would be delighted!" she said.

During mealtime, Caroline started to take the last of the scalloped potatoes, then said, "Dad, would you like to have the rest?"

"I sure would!" said Mr. Malloy. "*Thank* you, Caroline!"

Upstairs later, when Eddie and Beth were studying for final exams, Caroline stopped in Beth's doorway and whispered, "I was going to play my new CD, Beth, but I won't if you think it might bother you."

Then she moved across the hall to Eddie's room and

said, "If you need any pencils sharpened, just let me know."

"Knock it off, Caroline," said Eddie. "You're as fake as a wooden nickel."

"Well, I can *practice,* can't I?" Caroline replied. "If you haven't been nice for a long time, the only way to get nicer is to practice."

"Then practice on somebody else," Eddie said. "Go practice on the Hatfords, if you have to."

Caroline had been afraid someone would suggest that. She could do it, though. She *would* do it! There were only two more weeks of school before summer vacation began, and after that she wouldn't have to even look at the four Hatford boys unless she wanted to.

Caroline went to her room and sat on the edge of her bed. She looked out over the Buckman River, which came into town on the side of Island Avenue where the Malloys lived, ran under the road bridge that led to the business district, and flowed back out of town on the other side of Island Avenue.

It would be hard to leave West Virginia if their father moved them back to Ohio in the fall. Mr. Malloy was coach of the Buckman College football team for one year on a teacher-exchange program, and he still hadn't made up his mind whether he would stay or go back to Ohio. This was a bit unsettling to them all because no one knew where they would be come September. How could you get excited over moving on to a higher grade when you didn't even know what state your school would be in?

Caroline knew what the Hatford boys would like, however. They would like the Malloy girls to go home. They would have liked the Malloy sisters to go back to Ohio the week after they'd come to Buckman. They would have preferred that the Malloys had never come to West Virginia in the first place.

Why? Because the Malloys were renting the house where the Bensons used to live, and the five Benson brothers had been the Hatford boys' best friends. Jake and Josh and Wally—and sometimes even Peter Hatford—simply could not stand that three attractive, intelligent, talented *girls* (Caroline in particular) had taken the place of their best friends, Caroline decided, and they wanted the Bensons back.

Wally Hatford was the worst because Caroline had been moved up to his grade even though she was a year younger than he was. Could *she* help it if she was smart? Could she help it if she was precocious? *Get over it!* she would have liked to say to Wally, but she knew she was going to have to be nice. She was going to have to be so kind, in fact, that if her name came up on a list of possible helpers for the Strawberry Festival Parade, all pencils would automatically make a check mark in the box beside her name.

■

On the way to school the following morning, the Hatford boys were waiting for the girls, as usual, on the other end of the swinging footbridge that spanned the Buckman River.

Despite all their quarrels and tricks, the boys had

4

been doing this ever since a cougar had been seen lurking about Buckman and the two sets of parents had insisted that the kids all walk together as a group. Even though the danger was past—the cougar had been caught and transported to the Smoky Mountain area—walking to school together had become a habit. Much as the Hatfords and Malloys hated to admit it, they probably didn't dislike each other as much as they thought. There were times, in fact, when the boys *seemed* to wish the Malloys would *stay* in Buckman.

"Good *morn*-ing, Wally!" Caroline said pleasantly as she stepped off the footbridge.

"No," said Wally, his eyes straight ahead as he started toward school.

"No, what?"

"No to whatever you want me to do," Wally told her. He had a round face and a square shape, same as his little brother, Peter, who was in second grade, while the older twins, Jake and Josh, were taller and as lean as string beans.

"I'm not going to ask you to do anything," Caroline said. "I just wanted to show you that beginning today, I'm going to be about the nicest person you've ever met."

"What took you so long?" asked Wally.

"I've just decided to be a better person," Caroline explained.

"Better than who? You've *always* liked to be better than everyone else, Caroline," Wally told her.

Caroline decided she would not waste her time with

people who did not understand what a wonderful person she could be. She moved up and fell into step beside Peter, who was following Eddie and Beth and Jake and Josh. Peter was walking with his arms straight out in front of him and his eyes closed.

"What are you doing?" asked Caroline.

"Pretending I'm blind," said Peter, opening his eyes. "I want to find out if I could get to school by myself if I couldn't see."

"If you ever went blind, I would walk you to school and back every day," said Caroline sweetly.

"But that wouldn't count, because I want to do everything myself," said Peter. "I don't need any help."

How did nice people stay that way if nobody wanted them around? Caroline wondered. It used to be that she could count on Peter, at least, to be friendly.

"You're not mad at me, are you?" she asked.

"No, I'm just getting ready for not caring if you move back to Ohio," said Peter.

That's so sweet! Caroline thought. "Peter, I'm not sure *I* want to move back to Ohio either, but we can at least be friends, can't we?" she said.

"I guess so," said Peter.

"I'll even bake you some friendship cookies if you want," Caroline promised. Now if *that* wasn't nice, what was?

"With chocolate chips and raisins and M&M's?" asked Peter.

"Anything you want," said Caroline. "All you have

to do for me is put a little mark in the box beside my name."

"What box?" asked Peter.

"Well, if a list goes around town with people's names on it, people who might be chosen to be in the Strawberry Festival Parade, then I hope you'll think of the friendship cookies I'm going to bake for you and put a check mark beside my name."

"Okay," said Peter, closing his eyes and putting his arms out in front of him again.

"Curb, Peter!" Wally yelled behind them, just in time to stop Peter from stepping down into the street. "A lot of help *you* are," he muttered to Caroline as he moved beside her and guided his brother across the street.

Caroline felt discouraged. Wally wouldn't vote for her, that was for sure. So it was one vote *yes,* one vote *no.* She wasn't getting very far by being nice.

■ ■ ■ ■ ■ ■ ■ ■ ■ ■ ■

Two

■

Plans

Only two more weeks of school, Wally Hatford was thinking as he slid into his seat. Then he would not have to sit in front of Caroline ever again. She couldn't make Xs on his back any longer with her pencil eraser, or tap out a rhythm on his shoulder blades with her ruler. She couldn't whisper stupid stuff either, and try to make his neck and ears turn red.

Next year, if the Malloys stayed in Buckman and he was in the same class as Caroline, he would find a way to sit as far away from her as possible. If she was sitting in the front of the room, he would tell the teacher he was farsighted and had to sit in the last row. If Caroline was assigned to the back row, he would tell the teacher he was nearsighted and had to sit up front. Two more weeks, or ten more days, and he was a free man!

"Well, class," Miss Applebaum said from her desk, where a big bouquet of zinnias brightened the room, "I have news." She was wearing a yellow shirt, and green jangling earrings shaped like ears of corn. She always changed her earrings according to the season. "You all know that Buckman will hold its Strawberry Festival in three weeks and, of course, that there will be a parade."

"Yay!" the class said in unison.

"Strawberry pancakes!" said one of the girls.

"Strawberry shortcake," said a boy.

"Strawberry ice cream!"

"Strawberry milk shakes!"

"Strawberry sundaes!"

"But here's something you may not know," said Miss Applebaum. "The Buckman Community Hospital wants to build a whole new wing just for treating children. They'll have to raise a lot of money, and last week at the town council meeting, the mayor said it was a good idea to get children involved."

Wally knew that raising money wasn't quite the same as raising corn or lima beans, and certainly nothing like raising a puppy. *Oh, no!* he thought. *They're not going to get their hands on my piggy bank!*

"There isn't much time, we realize that," the teacher continued, "but we know you like parades and we know you like strawberries. So the First National Bank of Buckman has decided that all students who can earn or collect twenty dollars or more will have their choice of either all the strawberry treats they can eat or a place in the parade. Each of you can decide which you want."

"Parade!" someone said.

"Strawberry shortcake!" said another. "With whipped cream on top."

Wally couldn't make up his mind. He liked the idea of going from booth to booth for all the strawberry treats he could eat. Strawberry waffles with strawberry syrup, even. But he also liked the thought of riding on a float with a big brass band following along behind.

"And everyone who earns any money at all for the hospital fund will get a piece of strawberry shortcake," said Miss Applebaum.

"How are we supposed to earn the money?" someone asked.

"That's up to you, but you'll have to work fast," the teacher said. "The bank will provide the containers and you may want to go from house to house collecting money. Or maybe you can think of something you could do for your neighbors."

Wally knew that in every classroom in Buckman Elementary, every student was hearing the same thing from *his* teacher. Seven-year-old Peter down in second grade was probably hearing it right now, and so were his twin brothers, Josh and Jake, in sixth grade. So were the two older Malloy girls, Beth and Eddie. This meant that all three hundred and forty-two students could be out combing their neighborhoods at the same time, trying to collect twenty dollars for the hospital building fund.

"I know what I'm going to choose" came a whisper over Wally's left shoulder.

He knew he was supposed to turn around and ask, "What?" And when he didn't, the voice went on, "I'm going to ask to be on the float with the Strawberry Queen."

"Fat chance," Wally whispered back, turning his head to the side. If Caroline got to ride on the float with the Strawberry Queen, he was going to fly to the moon.

"I might even *be* the Strawberry Queen!" Caroline continued, her voice dreamy. "If I get to be Strawberry Queen, do you want to be Strawberry King and wave to the crowd beside me?"

Wally turned all the way around in his seat. "You aren't going to be the Strawberry Queen. You're not even going to be one of her servants, I'll bet!" He stopped suddenly because he was talking too loudly, and everyone was looking at him.

"Wally," said Miss Applebaum. "Maybe you and Caroline would like to continue your conversation at recess."

Wally faced forward again, the blood rising to his face as the other boys grinned. No, he did not want to discuss anything with Caroline at recess. He did not want to discuss anything with her ever again if he could help it. When the class spilled out onto the playground later, Wally and his friends started a game of kickball, and he was glad to forget Caroline for a while.

■

After school, he walked ahead of his brothers so that he was the first one to reach home. It was always a relief when the Malloy girls said goodbye at the footbridge and went on across the river to their house on Island Avenue. Then Wally could go inside his own house and close the door.

The phone rang as soon as the boys entered the kitchen. It was as though there were a surveillance camera above the stove and their mother, who worked in a hardware store, knew the minute they got home from school.

"Hello, Mom," Wally said, lifting the phone. He didn't even have to ask.

"Everything all right?" Mrs. Hatford said.

"Peter's been poisoned, Jake and Josh broke their legs, and Caroline gouged out my eyes with her ruler," Wally answered.

Mrs. Hatford ignored him completely. "There's some leftover pizza in the fridge you can have, along with the orange juice, but I don't want you boys eating anything else until supper," she said.

What would she say, Wally wondered, if Peter really *had* been poisoned? How would he ever make her understand it was for real?

"The kids at school are supposed to help raise money for the new children's wing at the hospital," Wally told her.

"I know. I heard someone talking about it at the store today," said his mother. "Have you thought of something you can do to earn money?"

Wally was watching his seven-year-old brother worm one finger up his nostril. He would dig around for a minute, wipe his finger on his pants, and dig some more. "I was thinking of selling Peter, but I doubt anyone would pay twenty dollars for him," he said.

"Go eat your pizza, Wally," his mother said. "And don't turn on the TV till you've done your homework."

Wally hung up and sat at the table waiting for the microwave to ding. He watched Josh pouring himself a glass of orange juice.

"Did you get the talk about raising money for the hospital?" he asked his brothers.

"Yeah," said Jake.

"You going to do it?"

"Sure. I've always wanted to ride on one of the floats," Jake answered.

"Me too," said Josh.

"*I'd* rather eat strawberries!" said Peter. "All the strawberry ice cream I can eat!" He rubbed his stomach in anticipation.

Jake looked around at his brothers. "Whatever we do to earn money, though, don't tell the Malloys. They'll just steal our ideas. Or else they'll think of some stupid way to make money and try to get us to go along with it."

"Yeah!" said Wally. "Caroline would probably write a play and want us to be in it."

13

"They'd charge everyone a dollar just to come and watch us act like idiots," said Josh.

"Eddie would be the worst, though," said Jake. "I'll bet she'd put on a baseball exhibition and charge people to come and watch her throw. Want us to stand out there and pitch balls to her just so everyone could see how hard she can hit."

Peter stuffed the last bite of pizza into his mouth and said, "Why are we mad at the girls? I thought we were friends now. I thought that after you and Eddie won the baseball championship, you were going to get along better, Jake."

The three older boys studied their brother.

"Who said we're mad at anybody?" asked Jake. "It's just time we started doing our own thing. If the Bensons move back this summer, we can't always be doing stuff with the girls, like bottle races down the river. They better get used to entertaining themselves, 'cause we've got a lot of catching up to do with the guys."

"Right. The girls have to learn to get along without us," said Josh.

Wally waited. He felt sure he knew what was coming next. He was positive he knew what Jake would say. Because where the Malloy girls were concerned, Jake always said the same sort of thing.

"Let's see who can earn the money first, them or us," said Jake.

"No fair!" said Josh. "There are only three of them and four of us. We should count Peter out."

"Are you kidding?" said Jake. "All Peter has to do is

stand outside a grocery store looking angelic, and people will be giving him money right and left."

"Put a halo around his head and people will be standing in line to ante up," said Wally.

They slugged down the last of the orange juice and sat back in their chairs, wiping their mouths on their sleeves.

"It'll be nice to have the Bensons back in their house again and the Malloys gone to Ohio," said Jake.

Peter tipped his glass back so far that it covered his nose. When the last drop of juice had trickled into his mouth, he put the glass on the table and said, "What if the Bensons come back and the girls decide to *stay*?"

Wally looked at Josh and Josh looked at Jake.

"That can't happen," said Jake, "because if Coach Benson comes back, *he'll* be coach of the college football team again, and Mr. Malloy will be out of a job."

"Oh," said Peter. The kitchen was quiet for a moment. "But what if Coach Benson doesn't *want* his old job back? What if he wants to do something else?"

"It doesn't matter what job he takes, Peter," Josh explained. "If the Bensons come back, they'll want their house back. And even if the Malloys stay, they'll have to move somewhere else."

"Yeah," said Jake, beginning to smile. "We won't have to see them crossing the footbridge every morning."

"We won't be walking with them to school," said Wally.

"We won't be wondering if they're looking at us

from across the river with their dad's binoculars, trying to see us in our underwear," said Josh.

"If they decide to stay in Buckman, they'll probably move clear across town," said Jake.

"Out in the country, even," said Josh. "It'll be like old times again. Just us and the Bensons. We won't even know the Malloys are around."

"*If* the Bensons come back, of course," Jake said.

To Wally, it seemed as though the summer were one gigantic *if.*

■ ■ ■ ■ ■ ■ ■ ■ ■ ■

Three

■

Bigger Plans

"So how are we going to raise money?" Beth asked her sisters after they'd crossed the bridge and started up the grassy hill to the house the Malloys were renting from the Bensons. "I think I'll bake cookies and sell them."

"I'd rather do something more physical—scrub porches or something," said Eddie. "What are *you* going to do, Caroline?"

"*I,*" said Caroline, who had been thinking about it all day, "am going to perform at birthday parties."

"You *what?*" asked Eddie.

"I'm going to wear costumes and act out fairy tales at little children's birthday parties. I'll wear a red cape for Little Red Riding Hood, a curly wig for Goldilocks, a snout for the Three Little Pigs—stuff like that. I'll be doing a service to the community and getting my name known around Buckman at the same time."

"How generous of you, Caroline!" said Eddie dryly. "But you'd better get a move on it. How many birthdays can there be in the next three weeks?"

They walked across the clearing toward the back door. "And we're not going to get stuck doing any projects with the Hatfords, right?" Eddie continued. "We'd end up doing all the work and they'd collect the money in their name."

"Don't worry," said Caroline. "I don't want any Hatfords messing up my act."

"Besides," said Beth, "we've got to start doing things with girls again, because if we go back to Ohio, most of our friends there are girls. Do you realize we've spent practically this whole year just hanging out with the Hatfords?"

Mrs. Malloy came downstairs carrying a basket of clothes for the laundry.

"Mom," Beth asked, "when is Dad going to make up his mind whether we're going back to Ohio or not?"

"If we are, he has to be back by August first to start football practice," her mother said, setting the basket on the table to rest her arm. "But you don't know your father."

"Well, if *he's* not our father, who is?" Eddie joked.

"What I *mean* is, he's tempted by every new offer that comes along. You'll never guess the latest!"

"What?" asked Caroline.

"Your dad got an offer to coach the Buckman High School football team."

"*High* school?" said Eddie. "Why would he want to give up being a coach for a college team to coach high school?"

"He says there's less pressure, less stress, and he just may like working with high school students for a change," her mother answered.

"But if we stay and the Bensons come back, we'll have to give up this house! We'll have to move somewhere else!" said Caroline.

"Exactly," said Mrs. Malloy. "Coach Benson will take over your dad's job again, your dad will start coaching the high school team, and I'll have to begin thinking of another house to rent until we're sure this is what your father really wants."

"But...but I *like* this house!" said Caroline. "If we stay in Buckman, I don't want to live anywhere else."

"Well, sweetie, I don't think you have much choice," said her mother.

"Do *you* want to go back to Ohio, Mom?" asked Beth.

"Part of me does and part of me doesn't," Mrs. Malloy said. "I miss some of my friends, but I've made some new ones here." She picked up the laundry basket again. "If we stay, we'll make it work, that's all. If we go back, well...that will be nice too." And she went on down the basement steps.

Beth sat at the kitchen table, her chin in her hands. "This is the pits," she said. "If we stay in Buckman, we can't stay in this house! We'll have to move clear across town, I'll bet, away from the river."

"Away from the Hatfords, you mean," said Eddie. "What's the matter? Going to miss Josh? I thought we wanted to get as far away from them as possible."

"Yeah," said Caroline wistfully. "Weird how guys who can be so much trouble can be so much fun to tease."

"I wonder what they really think of us," said Beth. "If we do go back to Ohio, do you suppose they'd miss us?"

"In a pig's eye," said Eddie. "The minute our car's out of sight, they'll throw a party to celebrate. *We're* the ones who ought to celebrate the minute we're outside the city limits."

The girls were quiet for a moment.

"Yeah, but we never had the fun of decorating boys' bedrooms with ruffles and lace," said Beth.

"We never sang a siren song through a trapdoor in a boy's roof, either," said Caroline. "We never had the fun of hiding a little boy in our house away from his brothers...."

More silence.

"You talk as though *we* might actually miss the *Hatfords!*" said Eddie.

"Ha!" said Beth.

"Never!" said Caroline.

■

Caroline went upstairs and carefully wrote out an advertisement on a large index card to pin up on the community bulletin board. She used four colors of felt-tipped pens: silver, copper, burgundy, and gold. She used three colors—red, yellow, and green—for the balloons she drew in each corner, and she placed a row of teddy bear stickers across the bottom.

Birthday Party Entertainment
Beautiful, talented girl will perform
for your child's birthday party.
Fairy tales, singing, dancing, and more!!!
All donations to go to the
Buckman Hospital Building Fund
Call Caroline Malloy

She wrote their telephone number at the bottom of the card and went over every word to make sure she had spelled it correctly. She was an excellent speller. Then she went downstairs. "I'm going to the library, Mother," she called.

"Be home in time for dinner," Mrs. Malloy answered from the kitchen.

Caroline went out the front door and walked down the long driveway to the road. The afternoon sun was still well above the hills outside Buckman and was warm on the back of her neck. Passing the other houses along Island Avenue, she followed the road to the bridge that led into the business district. Halfway across the bridge, she stopped and rested her elbows on the guardrail, staring down at the swirling water.

Only two months before, she had fallen into that

cold river and been swept along under this very bridge. Never mind that the water wasn't so deep she couldn't have touched bottom if she'd really tried. Never mind that she had caught hold of a floating branch and could have made her way to the bank.

She had gotten her name in the newspaper! When had anything like that happened to her back in Ohio? When had she ever gotten the chance to pretend she was dead and let her sisters slide her body into the water as if they were having a burial at sea? They had freaked out the Hatford boys, who had been spying on them from across the river that first day the Malloys had arrived. When had she ever done even half the exciting things she and her sisters had managed to do since they moved to West Virginia?

And—she had to admit it—it was all because of the Hatford boys. The boys had tried so hard to annoy the girls, hoping they would beg their father to move them back to Ohio, that the girls had decided to fight back.

The more the boys teased, the more the girls got even. The more the girls tried to get even, the more tricks the boys played on them. What on earth would they do for fun if they ever left this place?

■

At the library, Caroline went up to the desk and asked permission to pin an announcement on the bulletin board.

"May I see it first?" the librarian asked.

Caroline handed her the large index card.

"Why, what a nice idea, and what a thoughtful thing to do!" the librarian said after she had read it. "Of course you may pin it up, but I'm afraid that some of the parties might already have been planned. If I hear of any more birthdays coming along before the festival, though, I'll suggest that people call you."

"Thank you," said Caroline, feeling so noble and generous and kind and wonderful that she removed three other announcements to make room for her own. She thumbtacked hers right in the center of the bulletin board and squeezed the others into the corners.

After she left the library, she had not gotten halfway back to the bridge when she heard someone call her name. She turned and saw Wally Hatford coming out of Oldakers' Bookstore with a couple of comic books in his hand.

"Hey!" he yelled again, and that was a surprise, because it was usually Caroline who talked to Wally, not the other way around.

"Guess what?" he said, hurrying to catch up with her. "Have you heard the news?"

"What news?" Caroline asked.

"Dad just told us!" Wally said excitedly. "The Bensons are moving back to Buckman for real, and Coach Benson is going to take over his old job at the college again."

"How wonderful," Caroline said flatly.

Wally didn't stop there, however. "You know what

that means, don't you?" he continued with a grin. "That means your dad won't be coach there anymore, and you guys will have to move."

He just wouldn't stop grinning. *You'd think it was Christmas or something and he'd just been handed a present,* Caroline thought. "Well, you know what else?" she said, struggling to sound sweet. "*My* father has been offered the job of coaching the Buckman *high* school football team next year, so we just might decide to *stay* in Buckman. Now wouldn't *that* be terrific!"

They had reached the road bridge, and Caroline started across. Out of the corner of her eye she could see Wally staring speechlessly after her before he turned and walked rapidly down College Avenue toward his house.

■ ■ ■ ■ ■ ■ ■ ■ ■ ■ ■

Four

■

Horse Manure

Wally marched up the front steps of the Hatford house and into the living room, his eyes as round as walnuts. His dad was still in his United States Postal Service uniform, reading the newspaper on the couch right where he had been when Wally left.

"Where'd you go? Out to tell the world that the Bensons are coming back?" his father asked, turning to the sports section.

"Only Caroline," Wally said. "Where are Jake and Josh?"

"Upstairs, I imagine," said his father.

"Is that you, Wally?" Mrs. Hatford called from the kitchen. "Wash up now. We're about to eat."

Wally bounded up the stairs two at a time and into the bedroom where Jake and Josh were sitting at their computer, playing a video game. The twins had the new computer, of course. The old one was in Wally's room.

"Did you hear the news?" Wally panted.

Neither Jake nor Josh turned around. "Of course! The Bensons are coming back!" said Josh, still not taking his eyes off the game. "Dad already told us. You heard him."

"I mean the *bad* news," said Wally. "The Malloys might stay."

The twins turned their heads at the same time, as though their necks were electronically controlled.

"What?" said Jake.

"How do you know?" asked Josh.

"Caroline just told me. I saw her as I was coming out of the bookstore. Mr. Malloy might coach the *high* school football team next year," said Wally.

"No!" yelled Jake. "*I* wanted to go out for football when I got to high school. He'll remember every trick we played on the girls and bench me every game, I'll bet."

"This means . . . they'll stay in Buckman!" said Josh, stunned.

"Yep!" said Wally. "For*ever*, maybe! It means that Eddie and Beth and Caroline will grow up here and get married—maybe even marry our best friends—and have children who act just like them!"

"Dinner!" Mrs. Hatford called from downstairs.

Instead of the usual pounding of feet on the stairs, the three boys descended as though they were walking to a funeral. Peter had already washed his hands and had made it to the table before them.

Mrs. Hatford set the baked chicken and rice on the table with a bowl of creamed peas and onions.

"Ah, you know it's summer when we get the first fresh peas of the season!" said Mr. Hatford.

"Well, not quite," said his wife. "These came from the supermarket and were probably shipped in from somewhere else. But it won't be long before we'll be getting them from our own garden. Wally, would you start the asparagus around, please? Peter, help yourself to the bread."

"Only nine more days of school!" Peter said as he buttered his slice. "And then—va-*ca*-tion! Aren't you excited, Wally?"

"Yeah," Wally said flatly.

Mr. Hatford looked amused. "You don't *sound* excited. Are you going to miss your teacher over the summer?"

"No way!" said Wally.

"It's just that every time something *good* happens, something *bad* always follows," said Jake.

"Now, what in the world makes you think that?" asked his mother. "Sometimes something good happens and then something even better happens after that."

"Ha!" said Josh.

"So what awful thing could it be?" asked Mr.

Hatford. "I thought you guys would be excited that the Bensons are coming back."

"We are, except that the Malloys might stay after all," said Josh, and told his father about Coach Malloy.

"That's interesting," said Mr. Hatford. "Most high school coaches would rather teach college."

"Unless he's tired of living in a fishbowl," said Mrs. Hatford. "Everybody watches the college faculty, every move they make. It must be awful. I don't know how Jean and George stand it."

"Where would they live if they stayed?" Josh asked. "They'll have to leave the Bensons' house."

"They could move in with us!" Peter said helpfully, smiling around the table. "The girls could bake cookies for us!"

"Are you nuts?" yelped Jake.

"Caroline's going to bake cookies for *me*!" Peter crowed, his mouth full. "She's going to bake me some friendship cookies, and all I have to do is put a mark in a box by her name."

Mr. Hatford stared at his youngest son. "Come again?"

"Caroline said if I vote for her, she'll bake friendship cookies for me and then she'll get to be in the parade."

"Ha! Anyone can be in the parade if they collect twenty dollars for the hospital," said Wally.

"Only *I'm* not going to choose the parade when I get *my* twenty dollars!" said Peter. "*I'm* going to choose to have all the strawberry treats I can eat."

His father laughed. "Sounds to me as though you're

going to choose to have the biggest stomachache you've ever had," he said. "Pass the bread again, Wally, would you?"

Wally mechanically reached out and passed the bread. Then, like a robot, he passed the peas and the rice. He would have passed the chicken if his mother hadn't stopped him.

"Helloooo!" she said, waving one hand in front of his face. "If the girls stay in Buckman, it's not the end of the world, Wally."

■

After dinner the boys sat out on the front steps in the early June evening and watched the fireflies flitting about in the tall weeds between the road and the river.

"It may not be as bad as we think," Josh said, trying to find some good in the situation. "You *know* we'd miss the Malloys a *little* if they moved. Do you remember the time we howled outside their windows and scared them half to death?"

Jake grinned. "And tapped on the water pipes in their basement to make them think the house was haunted?"

"And the time we trapped Caroline in the cellar at Oldakers' Bookstore?" Josh chuckled.

"The fact is, they won't be in the Bensons' house, so why should we care if they stay or not? We'll probably be busy with the Bensons and won't see the girls at all. We'll only read about them in the paper when they get married or something," said Jake.

"Yeah, and Caroline will move away before any of

them, because *she* wants to live in New York City!" said Wally. "*She* wants to be on Broadway." He was beginning to feel better, and so were his brothers. They stretched out on the steps and put their hands behind their heads, looking up at the night sky.

"So how are we going to collect twenty dollars each before they do, that's what I want to figure out," said Jake.

"Are we sure we want to do all that work?" asked Josh.

"*I'd* like to ride on a float with a brass band following along behind," said Wally.

"Ha! Nobody promised we could ride on a float," said Josh. "They just said that if we collected twenty dollars or more, we could be in the parade. They didn't say we'd ride on anything. We could be assigned to walk behind a horse and sweep up manure, for all we know."

Wally's eyes opened wide. "They *wouldn't*!"

"Well, somebody's got to do it. They always have a few policemen on horseback at every parade, and there's always someone following along behind with a broom and a bag. You know that," Jake told him. " 'Earn twenty dollars and shovel up horse manure!' How's that for a reward?"

"*I* don't want to shovel horse manure! I want to eat strawberries!" said Peter.

"Yeah, and how are you going to earn the money?" asked Josh.

"I'm just going to stand downtown on a corner, hold

out my collection can, and say, 'Save a child! Save a child!' " Peter said. "No one can walk on by a boy who's saying 'Save a child.' "

Jake looked at his brothers and grinned. "He just might be right."

"Well, I guess I'll sit outside the library and try to sell some of my sketches," said Josh. "I don't know if anyone will buy them or not."

"Maybe I'll offer to mow lawns," said Jake. "What are you going to do, Wally?"

"I'm thinking, I'm thinking," Wally said.

Five

■

Onstage

When Caroline got home from the library, she went straight out to the kitchen, where Beth and Eddie were setting the table for dinner.

"The sky is falling," she said.

Mrs. Malloy turned from the stove, one hand on her hip. "Translation, Caroline?"

"The Bensons are definitely coming back. I heard it from Wally."

"So what else is new? We were pretty sure they would," said Eddie.

"No, we weren't. They kept saying that maybe Coach Benson would take a job down there in Georgia," said Caroline.

"Well, I'm not surprised," said her mother. "This just means I've really got to start looking around at houses for rent in case we stay. Meanwhile, if we're here for the summer, what do you girls have in mind? I don't want you moping around with nothing to do."

"I signed up for the mystery book club at the library," said Beth. "And Eddie's playing summer baseball." She turned to Caroline. "What about you?"

"*I* just might have a job," said Caroline. "I might go on performing at birthday parties all summer long. If I do, I can always say that I had my first acting job when I was nine years old."

"Oh, puh-*leeze*!" said Eddie, and clunked a handful of forks on the table.

■

The following day when Caroline got home from school, her mother said, "Someone called about a birthday party, Caroline. They want you to act out a fairy tale on Friday after school. The number's there by the phone."

Caroline clapped her hands excitedly, but then her face fell. "Only *one* call?" she asked. She had thought she'd get a dozen at least! Beth and Eddie rolled their eyes.

"Once word gets around, Caroline, the phone will ring off the hook," said Eddie.

"Yeah. There'll be a line halfway around the block, wanting to sign you up," said Beth, opening the cupboard and reaching for the pretzels.

Caroline cleared her throat and picked up the

phone. She dialed the number. When a woman answered, she said, "This is the actress Caroline Lenore Malloy calling about my performance at your party."

Her sisters groaned.

"Oh, yes," said the woman on the line, sounding a little surprised. "We live right across the street from the college. We'd like you to act out a fairy tale for some six-year-old girls. Could you do 'Hansel and Gretel'? It's my daughter's favorite."

"Of course," said Caroline.

"Friday at four-thirty," the woman said, and gave her the address. "Will five dollars be about right?"

"Yes, thank you. The money goes to the Hospital Building Fund, you know."

"Yes, that's lovely," said the woman.

As soon as she hung up, Caroline raced upstairs. She went through her closet looking for everything she might use as a costume for her fairy tales—a long black skirt, a red jacket, a fur-trimmed parka, a velvet dress with a lace collar.

She would have to be three different characters for this performance, she decided: Hansel, Gretel, and the witch. For Hansel's part, she borrowed Eddie's baseball cap; for Gretel, she chose a blue shawl to wear over her head. For the witch, she got down the pointed black hat she sometimes wore on Halloween.

Then she wrote out the script as she would say it and made little check marks beside each point where she was supposed to put something different on her head. Oh, she was going to be wonderful! She hoped the woman would call the newspaper and ask a photographer to come over on the day of the party and take a picture of the performance for the front page.

■

"Well," Caroline told the boys the next day when they met the Hatfords at the end of the bridge. "I have my first job! I'm going to collect five dollars on Friday for performing at a birthday party."

"What are you going to perform?" asked Josh.

" 'Hansel and Gretel,' " she said.

"You'll make a great witch," said Wally.

"That's because I'm a great actress," she said, and heard Wally sigh. "So how much money have *you* guys earned so far?"

The boys didn't answer.

"Nothing!" Peter spoke up finally. "We haven't earned anything yet."

■

After school on Friday, Caroline carefully packed a small bag with all the props she would need for her performance. Mrs. Malloy said she could put just a bit of blush on her cheeks and a thin smear of gloss on her lips to keep them moist. Caroline decided to wear black pants and shirt so she could more easily go from one character to another in her story. Finally, with the address in one hand and her bag in another, she set off for the birthday party. She had no trouble finding the house with the birthday balloons tied to the gate.

It was a large old house with a wide front porch, where eight little girls were playing tag. Wearing ruffled dresses and socks, they raced around the wicker rocking chairs, leaped over small tables, jumped on the couch cushions, and ran in and out of the house, banging the screen door each time. One of the girls almost knocked Caroline over as she went up the front steps and rang the bell.

An exhausted-looking woman answered. "Thank goodness you're here," she said. "The girls are absolutely wild, they're so excited. I'm getting the cake and ice cream ready, so I thought it would be helpful if you'd do your performance outside."

"Outside?" gasped Caroline.

"Yes. The girls can sit on the grass, and you can use the porch as a stage, if you like. Unless you'd rather perform on the grass and let the girls sit on the steps."

What Caroline would have liked just then was to turn around and go home, but she reminded herself that actresses have to put up with all kinds of conditions. Why, actresses often performed before soldiers in the desert, or in theaters without heat or air-conditioning.

"I . . . I guess I can do that," she said. "But I'd rather do my performance on the porch and let the audience sit on the grass."

"Wonderful. I'll just throw out a couple of picnic blankets and the girls can use those," the woman said. She called to a little girl in a pink dress. "Marci, this is Caroline. Marci is the birthday girl."

"Happy birthday," said Caroline.

While the little girls gathered around Caroline and

tried to see in her bag, the mother rounded up some blankets and told the girls the performance was about to begin.

"Hey! Make a tent!" one of the girls cried as she grabbed a blanket, and immediately they draped the blankets over bushes and got down on their knees to crawl beneath them. Then they stood up again, and half the girls got under one blanket while half got under the other, and they ran blindly around the lawn, bumping into each other and collapsing in laughter.

Caroline knew she would have to work fast to get their attention, so she put the baseball cap on her head and called, "Gretel! Gretel! Let's go for a walk."

The girls didn't even hear, they were making so much noise.

"Gretel!" Caroline called more loudly. "Let's go for a walk!"

One of the girls yanked off the blanket and pulled the other girls down beside her. "Hey!" she said. "Look at that girl wearing a baseball cap."

The rest of the girls looked toward the porch.

"This is the story of Hansel and Gretel," Caroline announced.

"I already know that story," someone yelled.

"Yeah! Why don't you do *Star Wars* or something?" said someone else.

"Shhhhh," said Marci. "It's my birthday and I can choose anything I want."

"Right!" said Caroline. And then she said to the girls, "What's unusual about this story is that I will take the part of three different characters. Please make yourselves comfortable and the story will begin."

One of the girls lay back and pretended to snore, and the others laughed. But finally they sat at attention, their hair hanging down in their faces, their dresses wrinkled.

"Once upon a time," Caroline began, "there were a little boy and a little girl who lived near the woods with their mother."

"Why are you wearing a baseball cap?" one of the girls shouted.

How rude! Caroline thought. The audience was never supposed to interrupt! She had to be nice, however. "I'm Hansel," she said.

"You don't *look* like a boy!" the girl answered, and the others giggled again.

Caroline put one finger to her lips to suggest they be quiet. "Gretel! Gretel!" she called again. "Let's go for a walk!" Quickly she took off the baseball cap and placed the shawl over her head. "All right," she said, "but we're not supposed to go in the deep, deep woods."

Then Caroline was Hansel once again. "We won't. We'll just pick some flowers and come right back," she said, the baseball cap on her head once more. When she became Gretel again, Caroline hummed to herself and did a little flower-picking dance as she twirled down a path in the forest.

Back and forth, back and forth, from the cap to the shawl, Caroline went, as Hansel and Gretel talked to each other, and the little girls out on the blankets laughed when she dropped the cap once in her hurry to get it on her head.

They quieted down when Hansel and Gretel decided to go a little way into the deep woods after all, and were fascinated when Caroline took a cracker from her pocket and dropped crumbs along the edge of the porch to show how Hansel planned to find his way home again.

Then came the arrival at the witch's house, and as soon as Caroline put on the witch's hat and made her voice all quavery, the girls watched intently. Caroline played it for all she was worth—the stooped posture, the trembly voice, the evil smile.

"Don't go in! Don't go in!" one little girl called nervously as Hansel and Gretel started to enter the imaginary gingerbread house. Caroline's chest swelled with pride to think she had captured the hearts of her audience.

What other girl her age could perform outside, using a porch for a stage? What other girl could entertain eight noisy girls at a birthday party? What other...?

Suddenly the witch's words were drowned out by the roar of a lawn mower. *No!* thought Caroline. *This can't be happening!*

"We can't hear you!" the birthday girl called.

Caroline talked more loudly and the noise of the lawn mower seemed to be getting fainter and fainter.

Then suddenly it must have turned around and headed back, for the noise grew louder, then louder still.

Caroline carried on, but no sooner had the witch put Hansel in a cage than the lawn mower was almost right beside them, in a neighbor's yard. And there was Jake Hatford, mowing the grass of the house next door.

What was an actress to do? How could she make him stop until she was through with her performance? How could she do it without getting out of character?

Well, here she was, playing the part of a little boy in a cage, with a witch wanting to fatten him up.

"Help!" she screamed. The little girls stared as Caroline clutched the imaginary bars of the cage. "Help!" she yelled again.

She saw Jake look around. She saw him stop. He stared at Caroline up on the porch and she yelled "Help!" a third time. Jake shut off the mower.

"What's the matter?" he called back.

Caroline took Hansel's cap off her head and put on the shawl in its place. Then, in a high, childlike voice she cried, "What's the matter is that my brother, Hansel, is locked in a witch's cage and she's going to eat him up!"

"Yeah!" yelled the birthday girl. "And we can't hear with all that noise."

"Well, I've got a job mowing this yard," said Jake.

"Just wait till the story's over," a bigger girl called back.

Jake rested his arms on the handle of the mower as Josh and Wally came around from the back, carrying a rake and a bag for the grass. They stopped and stared too. Now Caroline had a *real* audience.

Bravely she continued the story while the Hatford boys grinned and whispered from the neighbor's driveway. Two of the girls got restless and began wrestling out in the grass, pulling each other's hair and pretending *they* were Hansel and Gretel.

People just didn't understand what actresses had to endure, Caroline thought bitterly. Not only did she have to perform outside with a lawn mower waiting for her to finish, but she had to perform all the parts herself.

When it came time for Gretel to push the witch into the oven, and Caroline—in the witch's hat—bent over to look inside it, one of the girls from the audience crept up on the porch and did it for her, giving Caroline such a push that she went sprawling on the floor. The Hatford boys bellowed with laughter.

"Ding, dong, the witch is dead! The wicked witch is dead!" sang the girl, taking over the stage herself.

Caroline picked herself up and faced the audience. "The end," she said, all too happy to have the ordeal over.

"Girls!" called the mother from indoors. "Do you want to come in for ice cream and cake?"

Caroline could not get her props back in her bag fast enough, for she had been shamefully and cruelly treated. As the girls pushed by her to get inside, the woman came out on the porch and gave her a five-dollar bill.

"Would you like to come in for some refreshments?" the woman asked. "Perhaps you could tell the girls another story while they eat."

"No, thank you," said Caroline. "I think we've all had quite enough for one day."

Six

■

Two for a Dollar

Jake was the first of the boys to earn money for the new wing of the hospital. He got ten dollars for mowing the lawn, and he gave Wally and Josh two dollars each for helping out. But although he went down the list of all the neighbors, and even the friends of neighbors, Jake couldn't find anyone else who needed a lawn mowed. All the other students of Buckman Elementary were trying to earn money too. For every lawn in Buckman, there were two kids wanting to mow it.

As for Wally, he couldn't think of anything he *liked* to do that would earn him any money. He could think of a lot of things he *didn't* like to do, but he didn't want to do them unless he had to.

"You could always be a shoeshine boy," his dad told him on Saturday before he went to work. "There's a shoeshine kit in my closet. Maybe if you took that downtown, someone would want his shoes shined."

It was an idea. It was better than washing windows or weeding gardens. Wally could only remember one time in his whole life when he had shined his shoes, and that was when his aunt Margaret had gotten married. He decided to go downtown with Josh and try his luck.

Josh filled a box with paintings and drawings he hoped people would buy. He was probably the best artist in the whole school. Whenever a teacher wanted a mural for the hallway or a new picture for the bulletin board or a decoration for a party, it was Josh who was called on to help out.

Peter said he would go downtown with his brothers. Each boy had gotten his clear plastic collection can from the bank. Each can had a slit in the top for money and could only be opened by the bank itself. BUCKMAN HOSPITAL FUND, it read on each can.

It was a beautiful June morning in Buckman, made all the sweeter by the fact that there was only one more week of school. Wally always liked the last week of school. Most of the end-of-the-year tests were over, papers had been graded and handed back, and teachers often saved something special for those last few days.

Miss Applebaum, for example, was reading another book aloud to the class, *Hatchet,* about a boy who finds himself alone in the wilderness with only a hatchet to help him find food and shelter. *Could I do that?* Wally wondered. If somehow he got lost in the hills of West Virginia and nobody knew where he was, could he stay alive for a week? A month?

"You coming, Wally?" Josh called, turning around at the corner.

"Yeah," said Wally, realizing that he'd been so absorbed in his daydream, he had fallen behind Josh and Peter. How about a hatchet and a tent and ten jars of peanut butter? He was pretty sure he could survive for a while then.

Kids were swarming all over Buckman with their collection cans. Someone even came up to Wally to ask if *he* wanted to contribute any money.

"If I had any money to give, it would go in my own can," said Wally.

The boys walked to the low wall surrounding the library, where Josh propped up some of his paintings that he had mounted on cardboard. He kept the rest in the box so they wouldn't blow away.

ORIGINAL DRAWINGS BY JOSH HATFORD, $1.00, read the sign. ALL MONEY GOES TO THE BUCKMAN HOSPITAL FUND.

Josh hoisted himself up on the wall beside his paintings, legs dangling. Wally set up his shoeshine station a few feet away. He had brought a box to sit on, as well as the wooden shoeshine kit. There was a slanted footrest on top of the kit where a person could rest his foot, and Wally thought he would invite each customer to sit on the wall and put a foot on the wooden kit.

Peter, however, went to the corner, and as each person walked by or crossed the street, Peter smiled, held out his can, and said hopefully, "Save a child? Save a child?" And always, it seemed, the person would drop money into his can.

Wally and Josh were a little embarrassed to try to snag people as they passed. It was one thing to say "Save a child?" It was another to say "Buy a drawing?" And it was something else to say "Shine, mister?" when Wally was not even sure he remembered how to shine shoes.

He opened the wooden box. There were three tins of shoe polish inside—one marked BLACK, one marked BROWN, and one marked OXBLOOD. *Oxblood?* Wally wondered. Who would ever call a color oxblood? He twisted the lid of that tin. The polish had a dark burgundy color. It could be the color of anyone's blood, Wally figured.

There was a soft rag in the box with dark stains on it, obviously the rag used to dig into the creamy polish and smear it on shoes. And there was a brush, which Wally remembered he had used to make his shoes really shine once they were polished.

"Shine, mister?" he asked a man coming down the sidewalk. "Only a dollar. And all the money goes to the hospital building fund."

The man smiled and shook his head, and Wally saw that he was wearing white sneakers.

Now that he thought of it, Wally had never seen so many sneakers in his life! Were people even wearing black and brown leather shoes anymore? There were white sneakers with blue writing on the sides. Gray sneakers with red stripes. Blue sneakers with gold writing. How was he supposed to shine people's shoes if no one was wearing black, brown, or oxblood?

Josh wasn't having much luck either. People seemed unwilling to stop and look through his box of drawings. Some stopped to look at his paintings of cars and tigers and basketball stars.

"Did you draw this?" they would ask. Or they would say, "You're a pretty good artist, aren't you?" They would take a drawing and drop in a dollar bill or a couple of quarters. Or they might drop in a dime and not take any drawing at all.

Josh turned his sign around and wrote, ORIGINAL DRAWINGS, *TWO* FOR A DOLLAR. Wally began to call, "Shine, mister? Only fifty cents."

From the corner, however, came the constant *clunk, clunk* of change dropping into Peter's collection can. After a while he walked over to the wall where his brothers were sitting.

"My arm's getting tired," he complained. "The can's getting too heavy."

"Poor you!" Josh muttered.

"Yeah. We feel *so* sorry for you," said Wally.

"Isn't anyone buying your pictures, Josh?" asked Peter. "Isn't anyone getting shoes shined, Wally?"

"Sure. Can't you see the line around the block?" said Josh. A woman was coming down the sidewalk just then, and Josh jokingly held his collection can over Wally's head. "Save a child? Save a child?" he chanted.

"Cut it out," said Wally. The woman walked on by.

A man came out of the bank building next door to the library.

"Shine, mister?" called Wally. "All the money goes to the hospital fund."

The man stopped and looked at his watch. "Well, I guess I've got time for a shine," he said. He sat down on the wall and pulled out a newspaper from under his arm.

Wally swallowed. The man was wearing a light brown summer suit and light brown shoes to match. Wally looked in the shoeshine kit. There was only one color of brown. Dark brown. But maybe it didn't matter. He took out the polish, the rags, and the brush. Then he lifted the man's left foot and set it on the footrest on top of the box. The man went on reading his newspaper.

Wally opened the brown polish and carefully smeared it all over the man's shoe. He used the soft rag to rub it in. Then he took the brush and rubbed the shoe hard till it shone.

When Wally lifted the man's left foot from the box and put his right foot there in its place, the man turned the page of his newspaper and glanced down at his feet.

"My shoes are two different colors!" he said. "What have you done?"

"It...it was the only color of brown I had," said Wally.

"You ruined my left shoe! What am I supposed to do?" said the man.

"Well . . . maybe I'd better do the other one so they'll both be the same color," Wally suggested.

The man was angry. "I guess you'd better," he said. He didn't read his newspaper anymore. He frowned at Wally as his right shoe was polished, and when it was done, he didn't put any money at all in the can. "I ought to charge *you* for ruining my shoes!" he complained, and stalked off.

"I'm really sorry," Wally called after him, but the man didn't even turn around.

Wally climbed up on the wall beside Josh. "This was a bad idea," he said.

"Yeah. Tell me about it," said Josh, shoulders hunched.

When an hour and a half had gone by, Josh took another sheet of paper and made another sign: ORIGINAL DRAWINGS BY JOSH HATFORD, FOUR FOR A DOLLAR.

At the end of the afternoon, Josh had earned a total of two dollars and seventy-five cents and Wally had earned nothing. Peter's can, however, was almost full, and he had to turn it in at the bank and get another.

■ ■ ■ ■ ■ ■ ■ ■ ■ ■ ■ ■

Seven

■

Help! Help!

The girls were having no better luck. Beth had spent all Saturday baking, but the neighbors who had welcomed gifts of cookies at Christmas had about all the cookies they could eat. Early Sunday afternoon, Beth went door-to-door with her tray of homemade cookies on one arm, her collection can ready, but found that other students had gotten there first.

"Oh, dear. I've spent five dollars on cookies already this morning," one woman told her. "I'm sorry."

Beth kept going till she got to the next block, where she said to each person who answered the door, "Twelve cookies for the price of ten?" And when there were no takers there, she told the people on the third block they could have twelve cookies for the price of eight.

"If I eat all the cookies and cupcakes I've bought so far, I'll look like a blimp," one man told her, but he put a dollar in her collection can anyway.

Because the cans could be opened only by the bank, the girls had to estimate how much they had earned. As they could see through the cans, it was easy to figure out how much money was inside by tipping them back and forth. But Beth didn't even have to do that. After having spent the previous day baking, she came home with only one dollar in her can and no cookies sold at all.

Eddie was having a hard time too.

"Scrub your porch, ma'am?" she'd ask at each house along Island Avenue, except that some didn't have porches. Then she would offer to wash windows instead, but no one liked the thought of her climbing up on ladders, so everyone said no.

By the time Eddie got to the third and then the fourth block, she could see other students ahead of her, already knocking on doors, with buckets and rakes and scrub brushes in hand, offering to do any job at all. She turned around and went home. Caroline and Beth were sitting on the front steps waiting for her, failure written all over their faces.

"It's not even that I want to be in the parade as much as I just want to show I can *do* it!" Eddie said, flopping down beside them. "I mean, who cares if I get to ride on a float or not? But if I'm *not* in the parade, it will show everyone that I couldn't earn twenty dollars, and when there's a competition, I want to *win*!"

"*I* just want to ride on the float with the Strawberry Queen," said Caroline.

"I wish you would shut up about the Strawberry Queen," Eddie said irritably. "Nobody promised you that."

"*I'd* just like to see what Buckman looks like from the back of a float," said Beth. "I've been *to* parades before, but I've never been *in* one."

"Then we'd better start thinking of a way to earn money, because performing at birthday parties and baking cookies and scrubbing porches isn't going to cut it," said Eddie. "We ought to figure out something the three of us can do together."

They tried to think of jobs they had *not* seen anyone else doing around Buckman.

"Car wash?" Eddie said suddenly. "I haven't seen anyone offer a car wash."

"That doesn't mean nobody's doing it," said Beth. "I suppose there could always be two car washes, though. What would we have to do?"

"Get out the hose. Put a sign by the entrance to the driveway. One of us will vacuum the inside of the car, the next will hose down the outside, and the third will rub on the cleaner and wipe it off."

Caroline looked doubtful. "Have we ever washed a car before?" she asked.

"I did once, that time we went through the mud on vacation," Eddie answered.

Mrs. Malloy came out on the porch with glasses of iced tea for them. "It's shadier here than it is out back," she said. "It certainly has turned out to be a hot one."

"We want to do a car wash," Eddie told her. "It's the only thing we can think of to earn money for the hospital."

"Car washes are a lot of work and they use a lot of water," her mother said. "But it's for a good cause. If you girls think you can handle it, I guess it's okay." And she went back inside.

That decided, Eddie made a large sign to post at the end of the driveway: CAR WASH AND VACUUM—$4.00. MONEY GOES TO BUCKMAN HOSPITAL FUND.

Four dollars sounded better than five dollars, she figured, and might mean more business.

The girls worked together to get things ready. Hose, rags, bucket, cleaner, window spray, vacuum, brushes . . .

"I'm tired already," said Caroline, but stared as a car paused at the end of the driveway, then turned in. "Hey!" she yelled to her sisters. "Our first customer!"

A man got out of the car. "Where shall I wait while you wash my car?" he asked.

"Go right up on the front porch and have a seat," Eddie told him. "We'll call you as soon as it's ready."

The girls were glad to have him out of the way. They didn't want him watching on their first job. They opened the doors of his car and picked up all the trash on the floor—gum wrappers and soda cans, leaves and pebbles. Then they brushed off the seats with a whisk broom and used their mother's vacuum cleaner to suck up the sand and dirt. After that they closed the car doors and turned on the hose.

"We need to do a really good job," Eddie reminded the others, "because this will be a rolling advertisement for the kind of work we'll do."

The words were barely out of her mouth when another car turned in. A woman stuck her head out the window. "How long will I have to wait?" she called.

Caroline looked at Beth, and Beth looked at Eddie.

"We'll get to you right away," Eddie called back, handing the hose to Caroline. She turned to her sisters and said, "You finish up here and I'll go vacuum her car."

Caroline was so eager to finish the first car and help with the second that she wasn't careful about where she pointed the hose, and as the lady stepped out of her Ford station wagon, Caroline happened to pass a spray of water over her head.

The woman shrieked.

"Caroline!" Eddie shouted.

"Oops! I'm so sorry!" Caroline said, looking at the woman's wet shirt, not realizing that now the hose was turned on Beth, who was cleaning a wheel.

"Caroline!" screamed Beth, rolling out of the way.

"Are you sure you girls can do this?" the first customer asked as he came to the side of the porch to see what was going on.

"Oh, yes. We'll do a really good job!" Eddie told him. And to the woman she said, "Please have a seat up on the porch and we'll call you when we're finished."

She grabbed the hose out of Caroline's hand and gave it to Beth. "You do the wheels from now on, Caroline," she said.

Caroline hated doing wheels. They were the dirtiest part of an automobile, and her hands got as dirty as the rag. She had smudges of grease on her arms and legs, and every so often spray from the hose drifted down on her head. She didn't much mind the spray because it was the only way she could keep cool.

A budding actress should not have to be doing work like this, Caroline thought. It was a shame no one else had called her to perform at a birthday party.

"How can it be that no other kids in Buckman are having birthdays in June?" she asked her sisters.

"Well, maybe they're having birthdays, but they aren't having parties," said Beth. "Or maybe they're having parties, but they're not having performances. Or maybe they're having performances, but they're not having you, strange as that may seem, Caroline."

Impossible, thought Caroline. Who would *not* want a talented, precocious girl who could become all the different characters in a story? Who would *not* want to say, after Caroline became an actress on Broadway, that they had known Caroline when she was just a little girl back in fourth grade and had seen her perform once at a birthday party?

"Ready!" Beth called to the man on the porch as still another car pulled into the driveway.

The man paid his four dollars, but when he slid into the driver's seat he yelled, "Hey! There's water in here. Didn't you girls close my windows?"

Caroline turned to look and saw a puddle of water on the floor on the passenger side. The window above the seat was open an inch.

"I...we...I guess we thought you did," Eddie said. "We should have checked."

"For four dollars, you need to do a better job," the man said, and drove away.

"We need more help!" Eddie cried. "We need someone to stand out on the road with a sign directing cars in here. We need someone to close the windows and pick up trash, someone to vacuum, someone to do the wheels, wash the windows, use the cleaner, polish and dry...."

"In other words," said Beth, "the Hatfords."

"I'm afraid so," said Eddie.

The driver of the third car tapped her horn impatiently.

"I'm coming, I'm coming!" Eddie muttered.

"Are you *sure* we want the guys over here?" Beth asked. "Do we know what we're doing?"

"I know that if we *don't* have some help, we're going to go out of business," said Eddie. "Caroline, go call the Hatfords and ask if they want to go in with us on a car wash."

Anything was better than cleaning wheels for the rest of the day, Caroline thought. She dropped the rag and went into the house. She knew how suspicious the boys were of any Malloy idea, however. She knew Jake would quiz her and want a contract, probably, stating that the money they received would be divided equally among them. She didn't have time to stand at the telephone arguing with them.

So she dialed the boys' number, and when she heard Wally say, "Hello?" she simply called feebly into the phone, "Help! Help!" And hung up.

Eight

■

Cleaning the Clock

The Hatford boys enjoyed their usual Sunday chicken dinner. They had just changed from their white shirts and blue pants to T-shirts and shorts and were thinking about going outside to shoot baskets when the phone rang.

"Hello?" said Wally.

Nobody said hello at the other end. Instead, someone who sounded remarkably like Caroline Malloy yelled, "Help! Help!" And before Wally could ask what was wrong, she hung up.

Wally walked to the doorway of the living room, where his brothers were reading the Sunday comics.

"Who was that?" asked Josh.

"I *think* it was Caroline," said Wally. "I *think* she's in trouble."

"Why? What did she say?" asked Jake.

"She just yelled, 'Help!' " Wally said.

"Help? That's all?" asked Josh.

"Actually, she said, 'Help! Help!' " Wally told them.

Peter jumped to his feet. "Then let's go rescue her. Maybe she fell in the river again!"

"Sure, she's calling from the river. Right!" said Josh.

"Don't be in too big a hurry to get over there. You *know* it's a trick," said Jake.

Wally was uneasy. "But what if it's not?"

"Yeah, what if there's a murderer in her house or something?" said Peter.

"On a Sunday afternoon?" said Jake.

"Murderers get in whenever they want," said Peter.

Wally thought they ought to go too, trick or no trick.

"Well, at least it will be more interesting than shooting baskets," said Josh. "Let's go."

The boys went outside and trooped across the footbridge, then up the grassy hill in the June sunshine. When they reached the clearing between the house and the garage, they saw two cars sitting in the Malloys' driveway and three girls trying to wash two cars at once.

"Help!" Caroline cried again when she saw the Hatfords.

"Who's drowning?" asked Jake suspiciously.

"*We're* drowning—in work!" Eddie told him. "We

59

started a car wash to earn money for the hospital, and now we can't keep up with all the cars turning in. If you guys will help out, we'll split the money seven ways." Even as she spoke, another car came up the drive.

It was better than nothing, Wally thought. Heck, he'd help even if his brothers didn't. Peter immediately picked up a rag.

"I guess we can do it," said Jake.

"I'll polish," said Josh.

It was sort of neat to form an assembly line, Wally decided. Caroline and Peter were assigned to the wheels, Eddie used the hose, Beth did the vacuuming, and Jake and Josh did the cleaning and polishing.

"What am I supposed to do?" Wally asked.

"You need to go to the end of the driveway, stand by the sign I made, and try to get cars to turn in," said Eddie.

Heck, he had the best job of all, Wally thought. *That* was a change. Usually he got the worst of things. How did he get to be traffic cop all of a sudden?

Wally walked to the end of the wide driveway and stood by the car wash sign. It was two or three minutes before any car passed at all. Finally a tow truck appeared in the distance. Wally decided that a tow truck would be unlikely to use a car wash, and he was right. Even though he motioned for it to turn into the Malloys' driveway, it sped on past.

Wally stood on one foot, then the other. He counted

to a hundred by fives, then by fours and threes. Another car came by, tooted its horn, and drove on. The third car, however, slowed down and turned in.

"Do you guys do a good job?" the driver asked.

"Oh, yeah!" said Wally, and directed him toward the clearing. There was space for four cars at once.

He wished he were wearing a traffic cop's orange vest. That would be neat—standing out here directing traffic, making the cars stop. Holding out the flat of his hand to stop cars in one direction, motioning the other cars right up the driveway. He'd even use his whistle. He would back them up all the way to the bridge just to let a car turn in at the car wash.

Wally tried counting to a hundred by sixes and sevens and eights. Another car came by and slowed.

"For four dollars, that's a bargain!" the woman said, and took her place in line.

Wally had just started to count by nines when he heard somebody yell, "Hey!" He turned around.

There were two boys from school walking toward him. Big boys. Probably fifth or sixth graders, and one was as big as a washing machine.

"You stole our idea!" said the washing machine.

"What?" said Wally.

The other boy pointed toward Eddie's sign. "Car wash. We did it first."

Wally shrugged. "I don't know anything about your car wash, but so what? Anybody can wash cars. I'm just helping the Malloys out."

"Well, you'd better stop. You'd better close up, because you're taking customers away from us," said the first boy.

"Where do you live?" asked Wally.

The boys pointed far down Island Avenue.

"What are you charging?" Wally asked, curious.

"Five dollars. Six to wash and vacuum. You're stealing our business."

"You'd better talk to Eddie Malloy, then. She's the one with the hose," Wally said, pointing her out.

The boys looked up the driveway to where Josh and Jake and Eddie and Beth and Caroline and Peter were all hard at work.

"We don't want to talk to Eddie, we're talking to you," said the washing machine. "And you'd better tell her to close up shop, or we'll come back and clean your clock."

"Yeah," said the other boy. "We'll clear your deck."

"Punch out your lights," said the washing machine, and they went off down the road. One of them turned and waved his fist in the air before he started on across the road bridge.

Wally waited a minute, then walked up the drive toward the twins, who were polishing the hood of a car.

"Somebody's going to come back here and punch out my lights if we don't close the car wash," he said.

"They're going to do *what*?" asked Eddie.

"Clean my clock and clear my deck," said Wally.

"Who were they?" asked Josh.

"Fifth or sixth graders, I think. One was as big as a washing machine."

"Gus Bradley," said Jake. "I'll bet that's who it was. He just goes around talking big."

"He *is* big!" said Wally.

"Well, you just go out there like you belong by that sign," said Jake. "And if they come back and start anything, you tell them you'll clean *their* clocks!"

"What?" said Wally. He had never won a fight in his life. He'd never even been in one, except with his brothers.

"You're not afraid of them, are you?" asked Beth.

"Heck, no!" said Wally. He was terrified.

"So just go right back out there and keep directing cars up the driveway. If they come back and tell you to close up, say, 'Try and make me,' " said Eddie.

Wally swallowed. One punch to the nose and they *would* make him.

He hunched his shoulders and went back to stand by the road. Another car came along, then stopped, and the man looked at the car wash sign. Wally waved him on in. Fifteen minutes went by. Another car pulled in. Twenty minutes...

And then, coming back across the road bridge was the washing machine. This time it appeared he had the dryer with him, because there was a third boy, almost as large. Three boys on sturdy legs who had the look of trouble about them. One was going to clean his clock, one was going to clear his deck, and the third was going to punch out his lights.

Why was it, Wally wondered, that even when it *looked* as though he had the best job of all, it was really the worst? Why was it always Wally who seemed to be in the wrong place at the wrong time?

"Hey, pipsqueak, you still in business?" called the washing machine.

"I thought we told you to close up," said the second boy.

"I think it's time we cleaned his clock," said the dryer.

Wally stood like a statue, his jaws clamped shut.

"So what do you have to say? Anything? You going to close down?" asked the dryer.

"Nope," said Wally, and wondered what a broken nose felt like.

"You mean you're going to stand out here and keep stealing our customers?" asked the washing machine.

"I guess we'll take whatever business we can get," said Wally.

The three boys looked at each other.

"I think he wants us to punch out his lights," said the third boy.

"I think he wants us to clear his deck," said the dryer.

At that moment there came a voice back by the car wash yelling, "War!"

Wally turned around. Down the driveway came Jake with the hose, Josh with a bucket, Eddie with a broom, Beth with a brush, Peter with a dirty, wet rag, and

Caroline waving a towel above her head like a lasso. They were hooting and hollering and bellowing and braying.

The three boys in front of Wally each took a step backward, their fists clenched, then stepped back again.

By the time the broom and bucket and hose and rags and brush reached the end of the driveway, two of the men customers had started down the drive as well. "Need some help?" one of them called.

The three big boys suddenly turned and began walking rapidly down Island Avenue, then faster still.

"Yahoo!" yelled Eddie.

"Look at them go!" said Jake.

"If they don't watch out, they'll trip over their own feet and punch out their own lights." Josh laughed.

With a huge sigh of relief, Wally went back up the driveway with the others and helped finish washing the last of the cars. When evening settled in over the neighborhood, they divided their earnings among their seven collection cans. As it happened, exactly seven cars had come by, which meant that each of them got four dollars for his collection can. It seemed like a lot of work for only four dollars, but they had to admit it had been fun.

"If we do this next weekend, I think we'll have it made," said Eddie. "You want us to deal you in?"

"Sure," said Jake.

And even though both the Hatfords and the Malloys had promised they would do their projects alone, it began to look as though they were going to be stuck together in this business like Velcro.

As the boys went back home across the footbridge, Jake said, "Don't worry. One more week of school, one more weekend of the car wash, and we're out of here. We can stay on our side of the river the whole rest of the summer if we want to."

■ ■ ■ ■ ■ ■ ■ ■ ■ ■ ■

Nine

■

Plane-Wrecked

The last week of school had arrived, and Caroline was as sorry as she was glad. Glad because she could put all her energy into planning for the Strawberry Festival; sorry because one of the pleasures of her life was doing anything at all in front of the class.

It didn't matter if she was only asked to put a problem on the blackboard or read aloud the next two pages of their literature book. She always managed to make it a performance. She never just read from her seat, either; she stood so that everyone could see her. If she knew she was going to do something special on a particular day, she would wear an especially pretty dress to school.

"Crazy with a capital *C*!" the other girls called her, but Caroline didn't care. They tolerated her because she was a year younger than anyone else, and besides, school would be twice as boring if Caroline Malloy weren't there to entertain them, and they knew it.

Miss Applebaum finished reading *Hatchet* aloud, and after she closed the book, she said, "Okay, class, here's a fun project for our last week of school. I want each of you to pick a primitive place anywhere you like in the world. A real wilderness. Research it here at school—you don't have to do any work at home—and make a list of all the things you would need to survive there for a month. Then write down what you would do first if you were shipwrecked or plane-wrecked at this spot."

Well, that's *certainly an unusual assignment*, Caroline thought.

The teacher went on: "You may work alone or in groups of two or three, and at the end of the week, after you've shared your report with the class, we'll have a survivor party here in the classroom."

Friends began turning to friends to see who wanted a partner. Caroline tapped Wally on the back with her ruler.

"Wally," she said, as nicely as she could. "Do you want to be my partner?"

"No," said Wally.

"I'll choose anywhere you want. We could even be plane-wrecked in Antarctica."

"If you go to the South Pole, I'll go to the North," said Wally.

"How about Tibet?" asked Caroline.

"If you go to Tibet, I'll go to the Amazon," said Wally.

Caroline sighed. Trying to be nice to a Hatford was one of the hardest things she ever did. She rested her chin on her hands, closed her eyes, and thought. She did not want to be cold, so Antarctica was out. She did not want to be hot, either, and she did not want to be in a jungle where lions and insects could eat her alive.

If she was ever in a plane wreck, she wanted to be *found,* she decided, and to be found, she'd need to be seen. For her to be seen, there would have to be open spaces. So Caroline chose the Australian outback.

She spent the afternoon in the library looking at a topographical map of Australia showing the highlands, lowlands, and lakes. At last she chose what appeared to be open land on the edge of a desert next to a lake. Then she looked up temperatures to decide what month she would choose for her plane wreck. She allowed herself to salvage a raincoat, a jug of water, and some apples from the wreck. After that, she put her mind to being rescued.

Wally had walked behind her chair in the library, she knew, and had seen her studying the map of Australia. She was sure that was why he picked the North Pole. He was sitting across from her now at a library table because all the other chairs were taken, and he was reading a short book about Robert E. Peary.

"Wally," she said softly, "if you were searching for me in Australia, what would I need to do for you to find me?"

"Come hopping by on a kangaroo," Wally said without even looking up.

It was *especially* hard to be nice to a Hatford when he wouldn't take you seriously, Caroline decided.

"If you were plane-wrecked at the North Pole, *I'd* come and rescue *you*," she said as sweetly as possible. But Wally didn't answer, and Caroline knew she would get no help from him. She decided that if her plane was too smashed up to use for shelter, she would use her raincoat to make herself a tent. The real problem was how to let rescuers know where she was.

First she would gather rocks from the riverbank to spell out her name, *Caroline Lenore Malloy*. If she was a Broadway actress when the plane went down, think what the newspaper headlines would say when a plane spotted her name spelled out in rocks!

When she tried to figure out how many rocks it would take to spell her name in big letters—*big* rocks, at least as large as footballs—she decided to leave off her middle name. And when she realized how many trips to the riverbank it would take to spell out her first name, she decided she would just go with the word *HELP!*

There was every chance, however, that if her plane went down in Australia, an Aborigine would see her.

He would tell someone else, and that person would tell another, until a whole tribe of Australian Aborigines would travel through the outback to see her. And she knew what *that* would be: an audience.

And once she had an audience, she would sing every song she'd ever learned, tell every story she'd ever heard, act out every part she'd ever played. And *then,* perhaps, the natives would tell the outside world where she was.

■

It was exhausting, doing all this planning, and by the time Caroline started home that afternoon with the others, she felt as though she had been carrying rocks from a riverbank all day long.

Wally told his brothers about the assignment.

"You're lucky!" Josh said. You know what *we* have to do, just because it's our last year in this school? *We* have to pick up trash on the playground, paint the seesaws, collect all the volleyballs and get them back to the right rooms, clean out the supply cupboard, wash the blackboard, and help check in books at the library."

"No graduation ceremony?" Caroline asked. She could not imagine leaving elementary school for junior high without a ceremony of some sort.

"We get our class picture in the newspaper, that's all," said Josh. "They always print a sixth-grade graduation picture along with all the stuff the class did for the school before they left."

That was a ceremony? Caroline wondered. If all they got in Buckman was a picture in the newspaper, she would arrange to be in the very center of the front row.

"So where are *you* going to be plane-wrecked, Caroline?" Eddie asked as the seven kids made their way down the sidewalk on College Avenue.

"The Australian outback," said Caroline. "I'm going to sing and dance and attract the attention of the Aborigines, and if that doesn't get me rescued, I'll send up smoke signals."

"Couldn't happen to a nicer person." Jake grinned.

"*I* don't have to clean out a supply cupboard or be in a plane crash or *any*thing!" said Peter. "*Our* class is going to have a picnic out under the trees and make our own ice cream."

Caroline almost wished she hadn't been moved up a grade. Not that she would have been in Peter's class, but it seemed that the younger you were in school, the more fun you could have. She was just about to say so when she stopped walking and said, "Hey! Isn't that Mom way down the street?"

Her sisters shielded their eyes from the June sun. "Sure looks like it," Eddie answered. "Is she coming out of your house, Jake?"

"No, she's coming out of the house next door," he said. "The Corbys'."

"She's heading for the footbridge," said Caroline. "Maybe she was out collecting money for us so we can all be in the parade."

"Dream on," said Eddie.

Josh must have been in an especially good mood,

because when they reached the Hatford house, he said to the girls, "Anybody want some lemonade? We made a couple jugs of it over the weekend."

"Sure," said Beth. "We'll have a glass before we go home."

If any one of the Hatfords would miss them if they moved back to Ohio, Caroline thought, it would be Josh. Next to Peter, of course. And Josh would miss Beth most of all, she was sure of it.

They all trooped inside. As always, they had barely got the screen door closed behind them when the phone rang.

"That'll be Mom," said Wally, and picked it up. "We just walked in the door, Mom, and the kitchen's full of crazy people," he said into the phone, looking at the Malloy sisters sitting around the table.

Caroline stared.

Wally listened for a minute, then said, "Yes, there's a key on the table...." And suddenly he started to yell: "What?" And then, after another pause, he yelled *"What?"* again, even more loudly. Everyone turned to stare this time. And then Wally held the phone out away from his ear so the others could hear too.

"Now, why should that upset you?" Mrs. Hatford was saying. "All I said was that if our neighbors aren't home when Mrs. Malloy comes by, she'll stop over here for their key and you're to give it to her. She's thinking about renting the house next door if they stay in Buckman."

■ ■ ■ ■ ■ ■ ■ ■ ■ ■ ■

Ten

■

Stunned

Wally silently followed the others out onto the porch to stare at the house next door. He could see someone moving around inside, so the Corbys had been home after all to let Mrs. Malloy in. It was a big house, with a living room that stretched from one side to the other. He had known the Corbys were planning to move, but he hadn't thought they were going this soon.

He looked at his brothers in horror, then at the Malloy girls. For once he couldn't tell what they were thinking: they weren't frowning; they weren't smiling. Maybe, like him, they were in shock!

"Well," Eddie said at last, "thanks for the lemonade." Then she and Beth and Caroline went down the steps, crossed the road, and started across the footbridge over the Buckman River.

"This can't be happening!" Wally said at last.

Jake was frantic. "If the Malloys move in next door, we are toast!" he cried.

"Dead meat!" said Josh.

"Roadkill!" added Wally.

"It will be horrible," said Jake.

"Terrible!" said Josh, all trace of fondness for the girls gone in a flash.

Peter was eating a handful of crackers and stopped to study his brothers. "Why?" he asked. "What's the matter with the Malloys moving in next door? *I* think it would be nice."

Jake and Josh and Wally looked at each other, then at Peter.

"Peter, go in the house," Jake told him.

"Why?"

"Because I think your favorite show's on," said Jake.

"No, it's not!" said Peter.

"Okay, then. Because you can play my new video game if you do," said Jake.

"Okay!" said Peter happily. He went indoors, and soon the sounds of monsters and aliens filled the air.

"*Look* at it!" Jake said again, turning toward the house next to them. "It's got six windows on the side facing us!"

"And I'll bet all three of the ones on top belong to girls' bedrooms if the Malloys move in," said Josh.

"They'll see us in our pajamas!" Jake choked.

"They'll see us in our underwear!" Josh gulped.

"They might even see us in the bathtub!" cried Wally. "We'll have to keep our blinds down all the time and never ever let sunlight in our rooms. They'll know everything we ever do."

"When Dad gets mad and yells at us, they'll hear every word," said Jake.

"If one of us has to go to the bathroom in the middle of the night, they'll see the light come on and they'll know who it is!" said Josh.

They sank down on the glider facing the house next door.

"What are we going to do?" Josh said. "This is worse than having them living in the Bensons' house."

"There's only one thing *to* do," said Jake. "We've got to make sure the Malloys don't rent it—that they move somewhere else."

Josh began pushing against the floor with his feet. The glider moved jerkily back and forth. "Yeah? How are we supposed to do that?" he said. "Sit out here with a shotgun?"

"We have to make sure they don't *want* to rent it," Jake said.

"Don't tell me you're going to try to make them think it's haunted," said Wally.

"No, not haunted. Infested."

"With what? Ghosts? Bats? Mice? Squirrels?" asked Wally.

When Jake's eyes came together over the bridge of his nose, Wally knew that his brother's brain was working overtime—that he was thinking as hard as he possibly could. "Termites," Jake said at last.

"Termites!" said Josh. "How are we supposed to bring *that* off?"

Jake stood up. "I'll be back," he said. He walked down the front steps and disappeared around the side of the house.

Wally took a deep breath, held it, then said, "This is going to end awful, you know."

"What makes you think that?" said Josh, but he didn't look so sure of Jake either.

"Because they probably don't have any termites at all! I haven't seen any termites! Jake wouldn't know a termite if one sat on his nose. What are we going to do? Go on a termite hunt and give them a free ride to the Corbys' basement?"

Jake came back around the house just then, holding something in his hand. He gave it to his brothers to examine, and Wally found himself staring down at a narrow strip of wood that looked as though it had been out in the weather for twenty years. Green paint was peeling off one edge, and it was riddled with tiny insect holes. When Josh ran his thumb over one end, the wood crumbled in his hand.

"Looks like a piece of window frame, doesn't it?" Jake said.

"Yeah, but where did you get it?" asked Josh.

"From the Corbys' woodpile."

"And what are you going to tell the Malloys?" asked Wally.

"That it came from the Corbys'! That's the truth."

"This will never work!" said Wally. "It will never ever work!"

"Why not?"

"Because it's a lie."

"Who says it's a lie? I found it at the Corbys', and if they ask what it is, I'll say it looks like a piece of window frame. It does, doesn't it? It was lying on the ground. That's the truth too."

"It's still a lie," said Wally. "You're making them think it fell off a window frame, even if you don't say so."

Jake looked him in the eye. "Which is worse, Wally? Not saying the whole truth and living in peace and freedom, or explaining every last detail and ruining the lives of everyone in this house?"

Well, when he puts it that *way,* Wally thought. The boys were quiet awhile longer.

"So what exactly are we going to do?" asked Josh. "Go knock on the Malloys' front door, ask to speak to their parents, and say, 'This is what you'll get if you move into the Corbys' house'?"

"Yeah, what if they pick up the phone, call the Corbys, and *ask* if they have termites?" said Wally.

Jake tapped the stick of wood against the palm of his hand and moved his lower lip back and forth against his teeth, thinking. "We have to be diplomatic about this," he said. "Here's what we'll do. In an hour or so, about the time Coach Malloy comes home, we'll wander over to their house. We'll sit out on their porch talking to the girls and then...Well, leave it to me."

Gladly, thought Wally, because he had the feeling he shouldn't have any part in this whatsoever. It had the word *trouble* stamped all over it.

"There's just one problem," said Josh. "If Mom or Dad isn't home in an hour, we can't leave Peter here by himself."

"So we'll take him with us," said Jake. "Don't worry. He doesn't have a clue."

■

When fifty minutes had gone by, Jake told his brothers they ought to leave. He wanted to be sitting on the Malloys' front porch when Mr. Malloy drove up. Then he could just ask his question without making a big deal of it.

"What question?" asked Wally.

"You'll see," said Jake. "Hey, Peter! We're going over to the Malloys' for a while," he called. "Come on."

"I don't want to," Peter called back. "I'm in the middle of a game."

"Well, you'll have to stop."

"You *said*!" Peter protested.

Jake went to the door and stuck his head inside. "Look. If you stop the game now and go with us, I'll let you have it the whole rest of the evening after we get back."

"Promise?"

"Promise."

"*O*-kay!" Peter called. A minute later he came reluctantly outside. "What do we have to go over *there* for?" he asked. "I didn't think you liked the girls! One minute you hate them and one minute you like them."

"We never said we hated anybody," Josh said. "We just want to talk to them for a little while."

The four boys traipsed across the footbridge, their steps sounding hollow on the narrow planks, the bridge bouncing beneath them. When they reached the other side, Jake put out his arms to slow them down. "Now just walk up there real casual, like we're out for an afternoon stroll," he said.

"An afternoon *stroll*?" said Wally. "When do we ever go for a stroll? What's this supposed to be, a park?"

"Just act natural, that's all you have to do," Jake told him, and they started up the grassy hill.

Wally had never paid any attention to acting natural. Somehow his hands felt too big and his feet too small. He tripped going up the hill and wondered if his shoelaces were untied. It was easy to act natural until somebody told you to do it, he thought. And when you had the gut feeling you were making a horrible mistake, it wasn't easy at all.

Eleven

■

The Visit

After leaving the Hatfords', the girls didn't speak until they were on the footbridge going home. Then Eddie said, "I don't know whether to laugh or cry."

"What could Mom be *thinking*—renting a house next to the Hatfords?" said Beth. "I mean, why not rent a house next to a reform school? A prison? An insane asylum?"

"So what's there to laugh at?" asked Caroline. "I don't see anything funny about it at all."

A deep chuckle came from Eddie's throat. "You don't? You don't see anything funny about being able to turn out the lights in our rooms at night and sit at the window watching the Hatfords?"

"They'll pull down their blinds! You know they will," said Beth.

"Or they could turn out *their* lights and watch *us*!" said Caroline.

Eddie stopped chuckling. "Yeah, that's true."

"So if we move next door to the Hatfords, both families will have to keep their blinds down day and night. People will think there's a feud going on or something," said Caroline.

"Well?" said Beth.

They went up the grassy hill behind their house and burst into the kitchen, where Mrs. Malloy had just opened a cookbook.

"Mom!" they cried accusingly.

Mrs. Malloy looked up from the chapter on desserts.

"Why did you *do* it?" Eddie demanded.

"For heaven's sake, do what?" her mother asked.

"Go see the house next door to the Hatfords'! You're not going to rent it, are you? We don't *want* to live next door to those guys."

"I haven't rented anything," Mrs. Malloy said. "I don't even know yet if we're staying in Buckman. But I want to have some idea of what's available if we are."

"I can't think of a worse place to live," said Beth.

"Well, it's not as though we have a wide choice," Mrs. Malloy went on. "Most of the houses on the market are for sale, not for rent, and we're not about to buy a house unless we plan on staying here for at least five years."

"Five *years!*" Eddie howled. "I'll be almost through high school in five years!"

"If we live next to the Hatfords for five years, I'll probably be half crazy," said Beth.

"And if we're not crazy, we'll never see sunlight unless we go outdoors, because our shades will be drawn day and night," Caroline put in.

"I have never seen you girls get as dramatic as when the Hatfords are mentioned," Mrs. Malloy said. "One would almost think they were your boyfriends."

"*Boy*friends!" the girls howled.

"No way!" said Eddie.

"Well, there's coffee cake on the counter if you want to have some with milk," their mother told them.

The girls went upstairs and changed into shorts and T-shirts. After they had eaten their snack, they went out in the front yard and took turns pushing each other on the long rope swing that hung from the beech tree. When one girl sat on the huge knot at the end of the rope, her sisters pulled her all the way over to the porch steps, climbed to the top, and let go. The girl on the swing would soar out over the front yard, back and forth, back and forth, the heavy limb above her bowing only slightly with her weight. When the swing stopped at last, it was another's turn.

"I wish we owned this house," Caroline said. "I love this swing and this tree."

Beth took her place on the rope. "I like looking out my window and watching the river," she said. "I like walking across the footbridge to get to school. I even like the name of our street—Island Avenue." Her sisters pulled her to the top of the steps, then let go. "Why do the Bensons have to come back?" she wailed, her voice sailing out over the yard.

"Because it's their house, that's why," said Eddie.

They continued swinging and talking, swinging and talking. . . . What they were going to do once the Strawberry Festival was over, whether the river would be deep enough for swimming, how they had talked of climbing Indian Knob, and whether they should go explore the site of the old coal mine.

Eddie had just taken her fifth turn on the swing when she said, "Well, look who's coming."

Caroline turned around, and there, walking across the clearing toward them, were the four Hatford boys.

"Something's up," murmured Eddie.

"Look at the expression on their faces!" said Beth. "When they look *that* pleasant, it means trouble."

Caroline looked from Eddie to Beth. Who were they kidding? They *liked* trouble. They *liked* the excitement the Hatford boys stirred up. They knew that if they moved back to Ohio, their lives would be dull as dishwater.

"What's this? A social call?" Eddie asked as the boys stopped a few yards away and stood awkwardly, hands in their pockets.

"What are *you* guys doing?" Beth asked.

"Acting natural," said Peter. Jake poked him on the

arm, and Caroline knew Eddie was right. Something was up.

Jake looked at the girls and shrugged. "Just out horsing around. What are *you* doing?"

"Horsing around," said Eddie, and studied him quizzically.

"We're not keeping you from dinner, are we?" Josh asked.

"No. Dad isn't home yet," said Beth.

"What time does he usually get home?" Jake asked, and faked a yawn.

"Anytime now," said Eddie. "What's the matter with you guys? You want to be invited for dinner?"

"No!" said Wally.

"Yes!" said Peter. "What are you having?"

"Peter!" yelled Josh.

Jake went over and sat down on the front steps. Josh and Wally followed, and finally, Peter.

"It's a warm afternoon, isn't it?" said Jake.

"Yes," said Eddie.

"Warmer than yesterday," said Jake.

"Yes," said Beth.

"Probably as warm as it will get all summer," said Wally, trying to do his part.

"This is a boring conversation," said Peter.

"I agree," said Caroline.

Just then Mr. Malloy's car pulled in at the end of the drive, and the Hatford boys all turned in that direction.

The girls' father parked just outside the garage and, seeing the kids on the front porch, walked around the house.

"How you doing?" he said to the Hatfords.

"Fiiiiiine!" Peter warbled.

"I hear your car wash went pretty well Saturday," Mr. Malloy said. "Eddie tells me you're going to try it again this weekend."

"Yeah, but we'll do it at our place this time," Josh said. "Save some on your water bill."

"Well, that's thoughtful of you," said Mr. Malloy. "I'll vote for that."

He stepped between Peter and Wally to go up on the porch when Jake said, "Oh, by the way, Mr. Malloy, we thought we'd offer to paint the trim on the windows next door to us, and I just wondered if you knew how we should paint over this." He reached in his pocket and pulled out a stick of wood that looked as though it had been attacked by a woodpecker.

The girls' father took the stick and looked it over. "This from the Corbys' house?" he asked.

"Yeah. I just wondered how we should paint their trim—if you knew anything about painting."

"I don't know a whole lot, but if this is part of their window frame, I'd say it's going to take a lot more than paint. This looks like the wood's infested with something. Termites would be my guess."

"Termites!" said Jake in horror, gingerly taking the stick back. "That's pretty serious, isn't it?"

"Sure is. If I were your neighbor, I'd get my house

inspected by an expert," Mr. Malloy said, and he went on up the steps and then inside.

The girls looked at each other.

"When did you decide to do some painting?" Eddie asked, turning to Jake.

"Well, their house looked as though they could use it. It would be one more way to earn money."

"That's pretty hard work. How much are the Corbys paying you?" Eddie said.

"We haven't exactly come to an agreement yet," Jake answered, and threw the stick into the bushes as though he didn't even want it near him.

Peter looked from one girl to the other. "Are you going to move in next door to us?" he asked. "Is that what your mother was doing over at the Corbys'?"

"Anything is possible," Eddie said. "Of course, if we rent their place, there would have to be some conditions."

"What do you mean—conditions?" asked Wally.

"Well, when you rent a house you have to sign papers and have an agreement," Eddie explained. "I mean, the Corbys might say that we couldn't have pets and that nobody could smoke, and we couldn't hang heavy objects on the walls—things like that. And we could say that the neighbors couldn't shoot baskets after nine at night or turn up the TV too loud or have cookouts outside our windows—that kind of stuff."

"You could tell the *neighbors* what to do?" Josh choked.

Eddie shrugged. "You can put anything at all in an agreement," she said.

Jake took a deep breath. "Well, I don't think you'd want to live in a house with termites."

"Yeah," said Wally. "Some termite mounds are twenty feet high. I read that in a book. Just one termite mound could fill your whole living room."

"Oh, man! And do they ever bite!" said Josh. "I'll bet if a termite bit you on the cheek, your face would swell up like a basketball!"

Jake stood up and stretched. "Well," he said, "we'd better get home. We just thought we'd come over and tell you we can do the car wash at our place on Saturday."

"Sold," said Eddie.

"Goodbye!" said Peter. "Have a nice supper."

"We will," said Caroline.

The girls watched them go. "Those boys are so transparent you can see right through them," said Eddie. "That's the most far-out story they've come up with yet."

"How do you know it's not true?" asked Caroline. "It really did look like termite wood to me."

"Sure," said Eddie. "But it's not off the Corby house."

"How do you know?" asked Beth.

Eddie went down the steps and searched around in the bushes until she found the stick of wood Jake had thrown away.

"What color is this?" she asked her sisters, pointing to the peeling paint along one edge.

"Green," said Beth and Caroline together.

"And what color is the trim on the Corbys' windows?" Eddie went on. Then she answered for them: "Yellow."

■ ■ ■ ■ ■ ■ ■ ■ ■ ■ ■

Twelve

■

Alone on an Island

"**W**ell, that's that!" said Jake as the boys walked home. "They'll *never* rent the house now."

"I sure wouldn't want termites in *my* bed," said Peter. "It's nice of you to paint the Corbys' house for them, Jake."

"Uh . . . yeah. Sure," said Jake.

It did seem as though termites would put the Corbys' house at the bottom of the Malloys' list, Wally thought. Surely, if they stayed in Buckman, they would look at other houses for rent before they chose one with termites.

He turned his attention to the last project for school—where would he choose to be plane-wrecked?

He thought Caroline Malloy had chosen Australia, but she could always change her mind, especially if she found out he had chosen the North Pole. So what should he choose? Africa?

He imagined himself in a jungle. He imagined himself sitting under a banana tree. He imagined looking up and seeing Caroline swinging toward him on a vine. Nope. Not Africa.

The Sahara Desert, maybe? He imagined himself crawling up a sand dune looking for water. He imagined himself reaching the top and coming face-to-face with Caroline, crawling up the other side. Scratch the desert.

He could not imagine Caroline at the North Pole, however, so he decided to stick with that.

When he got to school the next morning, some people were checking maps at the front of the room. Some were looking through books at the back of the room. Others were going to and from the library.

Wally went to the library and spread out a map of the Arctic. It was very white. It was very empty. No roads, no cities, no lakes, no rivers. He closed his eyes and waved one finger around and around above the map, then let it drop.

There. Right there was where his two-engine plane would crash, about two inches from the spot marked NORTH POLE.

Wally decided he would use his hatchet to dig out blocks of ice and build himself an igloo. Unlike the boy in *Hatchet*, however, he would find a box of matches in the airplane. He could not see himself trying to start a fire without matches at the North Pole. And maybe he'd have a ham sandwich and a blanket, too.

First step: Get out of the plane in case it was going to explode.

"Hey, Wally!" a boy said. "I'm going to be shipwrecked off the coast of New Zealand. Want to be shipwrecked with me?"

"No!" Wally said emphatically. Too close to Australia.

"Well, don't get your britches in an uproar," the friend said. "I was just asking!"

The more Wally thought about Caroline, however, the more afraid he was that on the last day of school, she would announce that she had been plane-wrecked in the same place he had. Then everyone would say, "Oh, *Wal*-ly! How's *Car*-oline?" the whole rest of the summer. Or worse:

> *"Caroline and Wal-ly,*
> *Sitting in a tree,*
> *K-I-S-S-I-N-G!"*

It seemed that every time Wally unfolded a map, Caroline Malloy walked by his chair. Every time he got a book off the shelf, Caroline saw what it was. She was probably only pretending she was going to Australia, he thought. Whatever place he chose, he had to keep secret.

An *island*. That was the only place Wally could escape her, he was sure. He got a magnifying glass from the librarian, held it over a group of islands in the Pacific Ocean, and chose Banaba, one of the smallest islands he could find. It was so small, in fact, that Wally couldn't find out anything about it at all, and that suited him just fine.

Rainfall in the Pacific Islands varied from a few inches to many feet per year. Some islands were merely mounds of sand on a reef. Some were volcanic lava. Some had mountains and some had thick jungles. Wally decided his island could be anything he wanted it to be. But whenever he unfolded a map of the Pacific Ocean, he hid it beneath a map of the Arctic, just to fool Caroline. He absolutely would *not* go all summer with friends teasing him about being in an igloo with her, which was exactly what they would do if both he and Caroline chose the North Pole.

"Hey, Wally!" they would say. "Was it cold enough for you, or did *Car*-oline keep you warm?"

After school that day, the boys stayed behind a few minutes to help the music teacher load some instruments into her van. By the time they finished, the Malloy girls had already left, so the Hatfords walked home alone.

"Hey, Josh," Wally asked. "If you were stranded on an island in the Pacific, what kind of clothes would you wear? I have to know for my report."

"None," said Josh.

"None?"

"It would be hot! You'd be alone! Why would you want to wear clothes?" asked Josh.

Wally *definitely* did not want Caroline Malloy anywhere *near* his island.

As they got closer to home, they saw their neighbor weeding her lawn at the house next door to theirs.

"Hi, Mrs. Corby!" Peter called. "Jake's going to paint your house for you."

"Peter!" Jake snapped. "Shut up."

Mrs. Corby turned around and straightened up, bunches of dandelions dangling from both hands. "What?" she said. "Paint my house?"

Peter looked confused. "Well...I think he..."

"Shut *up!*" Jake muttered again through clenched teeth.

"*I* didn't tell her about the termites!" Peter said to his brothers.

"Termites? *What* termites?" Mrs. Corby said worriedly.

Josh clapped one hand over Peter's mouth, and Jake said, "We're just making up a story, that's all. Since you're moving away, we're making everything happen in your house."

Mrs. Corby looked doubtful. "Well, don't give me termites, not even in a story!" she said.

■

The phone rang when the boys walked inside, and Peter answered it. "Jake and Josh are mad at me!" he complained, ready to tell his mother everything. The twins clutched their foreheads. But then Peter stopped talking. "It's not?" he said. And then, to his brothers, "It's Beth."

The boys looked at each other. "What does she want?" Wally whispered.

"What do you want?" Peter said into the telephone. There was a long pause. "Uh-huh . . . ," said Peter. He listened some more. "Yes," he said. "Yeah, I saw her. . . . Uh-huh. . . . Uh-huh. . . . Uh-huh. . . ."

Wally and Jake and Josh all tried to get the phone away from Peter, but he had a tight grip on it and pressed himself against the wall. Finally he said, "Okay, goodbye," and hung up.

"What did she want?" the boys cried together.

"Why didn't you give me the phone?" demanded Jake.

"I can talk on the phone same as you!" said Peter.

"But what did Beth *want*?" asked Wally.

"She said, 'How are you, Peter?' "

"*Besides* that!" said Jake.

"She wanted to know if I knew whether or not Mrs. Corby was home, and I said yes."

"Why did Beth want to know that?" asked Josh.

"She said that she and Eddie and Caroline wanted to see the inside of her house themselves so they could choose their own bedrooms before they moved in," Peter told them.

"*What?*" Jake and Josh and Wally all yelled together.

"They didn't buy the termite story!" moaned Jake. "*Darn* it! Peter, when are they coming?"

Peter shrugged. "Soon, I guess."

Jake continued staring at Peter as though he were looking straight through him. Then he grabbed the Yellow Pages, leafed through them quickly, and dialed a number.

Wally knew when Jake lowered his voice that he was trying to sound grown-up. "Hello," Jake said. "I wondered if you had a truck in the College Avenue area. You do free inspections, don't you?"

Wally covered his eyes.

"Yes," Jake went on. "I'd like you to take a look at our house and the house next door." And he gave the address. "Sure.... Okay, that's fine.... Yes, that's terrific!" And he hung up.

"Jake, what are you *doing*?" said Josh.

"Desperate times call for desperate measures," said Jake. "The Malloys don't believe me about the termites."

"So what?" said Wally. "We don't believe you either!"

"So they'll move in!" said Jake. "They'll spy on us and make our lives miserable. All I want is for a termite company truck to be parked outside when the girls come over. That's all I ask."

This was a bad idea, Wally knew. This was a terrible idea!

"Well, if you think *I'm* going to answer the door and lie about termites in Mrs. Corby's house, you're nuts!" he said, knowing the way Jake always tried to pass the dirty work on to him.

"Nobody has to lie. *I* didn't lie either, did I? I just

said I wanted an inspection of our house and the house next door. It's free. I could even have done the Corbys a favor if the inspector finds something."

"What are we going to *say* when a truck gets here, Jake?" asked Josh. "Where do we think there are termites?"

"We don't have to say anything because we're not going to be here," Jake explained. "When we see the truck pull up, we're going to slip out the back door and hide in the toolshed till it's gone. The driver will walk around inspecting the outside of the house and then go over to Mrs. Corby's, and that's all the girls have to see. *Then* they'll believe there are termites, and they'll tell their folks. The driver will drive away, and that's all there is to it. The end."

The end, my foot! Wally thought. Mrs. Corby would find out they'd fibbed, and the termite truck driver would chase them to the ends of the earth. And as if that weren't enough, Wally just knew that Caroline was going to follow him to his island in the Pacific.

■ ■ ■ ■ ■ ■ ■ ■ ■ ■ ■ ■

Thirteen

■

A Bad Idea

"We'll shake them up," said Eddie. "Jake thinks he can fool us with that old stick of termite wood. All we're going to do is knock on Mrs. Corby's door and tell her we want to see the bedrooms—that Mom was over there yesterday to look at the house, and we just wondered what our bedrooms would be like."

"Gosh, Eddie, I don't know...," said Beth.

"What harm could it do? I'm not telling her we *are* renting her house. We're just taking a look, and we want the guys to watch us go in. Can't you just *see* Jake's face! We'll tell him later that we have our rooms all picked out."

Caroline giggled. "Maybe we should bring Dad's

binoculars and look into the Hatfords' upstairs windows while we're over there."

"Yeah! Bring those too!" said Eddie, and the girls laughed out loud.

A note from their mother on the table said she was shopping.

The girls ate some cheese crackers and drank some orange juice. Then Eddie said, "Let's go. We'd better get back before Mom comes home."

"You do the talking," Beth told her as they walked down the hill toward the bridge. "I don't want to lie."

"Who's lying? All I'm telling Mrs. Corby is we'd like to see the bedrooms. We would!"

Caroline was simply happy to go along. She was putting so much work into her Australian project that she was glad to get away. She had even made a watercolor painting of what an Australian hillside would look like with *HELP* spelled out in rocks, her little shelter made out of a raincoat off to one side.

She didn't know why Wally was being so secretive about *his* choice. Every time she looked his way, he had some other book tucked inside a book on the Arctic, and all the while he was really planning to be shipwrecked on a Pacific island. Why did *she* care where he was shipwrecked? Did he think she was going to follow him there? Just for that, maybe she *should*!

The girls were halfway across the footbridge when Caroline said, "Look at that! What *is* it?"

Her sisters looked. On the other side of the river, halfway between the Hatfords' house and the Corbys' next door, sat a white truck with a huge fiberglass insect on top. The big insect had a tapered body, wings, and terrible eyes and pincher jaws. TERMITE X, it said on the side of the truck.

"What's the *X* for?" asked Caroline.

"Death," said Eddie. "It means death to termites."

"Then it's true?" said Beth. "The house next door really *is* full of termites? I'm sorry for the Corbys, but I'm glad for us, because I *know* Mother wouldn't rent their place now."

"Yeah, but how do we pretend we're still interested in those bedrooms if they've got termites?" said Caroline.

"Look. We told Peter we were coming over to look at the house next door. So we're *going* to look at the house next door!" said Eddie. "We just know he'll tell his brothers."

They passed the Hatfords' house and went up the walk to the Corbys'. Eddie rang the bell. A few moments later a gray-haired woman in a blue sundress answered. "Hello?" she said.

"Hi. We're Mrs. Malloy's daughters, and I think she looked at your house yesterday," Eddie said.

"Oh, yes, she did!" Mrs. Corby's face brightened. "Have you decided to rent it after all?"

"Well, not exactly," said Eddie. "But we just wanted to see the bedrooms, in case we move in here."

"Certainly!" Mrs. Corby said, holding the door open. "Please come in."

And when the girls were inside she said, "The bedrooms used to belong to my children, you know. But they're all grown up and married." She started up the stairs, the girls following. "I've got bad knees, so this house is a little too much for me anymore. My husband and I are planning to move closer to our daughter in Elkins."

She held on to the banister as she climbed and stopped to catch her breath when they reached the top. Everything looked dark and old, and there was a certain mystery to the house. Caroline thought of all sorts of things she might explore if she lived here—cupboards to open, an attic to investigate.

"There are two bedrooms on this side of the hall and two on the other," Mrs. Corby said. "The bathroom's at the end."

Sure enough, two of the rooms looked directly toward the Hatfords'. As they peeked out the windows, the girls saw the Termite X driver in his white jumpsuit walking around the Hatfords' house, looking it over. The boys were nowhere in sight. Caroline even used the binoculars when Mrs. Corby wasn't watching, but she still couldn't see them.

"Well," Eddie said. "Thank you so much. You must really love this house."

"Oh, I do, and I'll hate to leave it," Mrs. Corby said, going back downstairs beside them. She told them to be sure to look at the flower beds as they left. "And please tell your mother I know she'll love the house as much as we do," she added.

As the girls opened the front door, they almost

bumped into the Termite X driver coming up the steps.

"Excuse me, ma'am," he said to Mrs. Corby, "but would you happen to be the person who called about termites in your house?"

"Termites!" Mrs. Corby said. "What *is* all this about termites?"

"I don't know, ma'am. My dispatcher told me to check out this house and the one next door, but no one's home over there."

"Well, I want you to know there are no termites in *this* house!" Mrs. Corby said. "And I don't appreciate your implying that there are."

"I'm only telling you what the dispatcher told me, ma'am," the driver said. "Sorry to have bothered you." And he went back to his truck and drove away.

"What do you suppose *that* was all about?" Eddie asked her sisters as they went down the sidewalk. "You don't suppose the Corbys really *do* have termites, do you?"

"And where do you think the guys went?" said Beth. "We wanted them to see us go in."

They walked back across the bridge, then up the bank and on up the grassy hill to their house. Mrs. Malloy was standing on the back porch, hands on her hips, waiting for them.

"Uh-oh," said Caroline.

"Just what have you girls done?" their mother said, and she sounded angry.

"Wh—what do you mean?" asked Eddie.

"I called Mrs. Corby this morning and told her that we'd decided against renting her house, and now you girls go over there to look at her bedrooms! What got into you? She has her hopes up again and thinks I've changed my mind. She just called and said you had only looked at two of the bedrooms and missed the most charming one of all."

Caroline could hear Eddie swallow as they started timidly up the back steps.

"I didn't know what to say!" Mrs. Malloy went on. "She was so disappointed when I told her there must be some mistake, but we had definitely decided we didn't want to live so close to the river."

"Well, I . . . ," Eddie began. "We might . . . We didn't know if you were going to take it or not, and in case you did, we wanted to see what our bedrooms would be like."

"I wish you would *ask* me before you do something like this!" Mrs. Malloy went on, following the girls inside.

"I'm sorry," Eddie said meekly.

"Well, you *should* be!" said her mother. The phone rang just then, and Mrs. Malloy picked it up. "Hello?" she said. She stood for a moment without saying anything, her eyes wide with astonishment. Then she slowly put the phone back down.

"Wh—who was that?" asked Caroline, almost afraid to know.

"That was Mrs. Corby again. She simply said, 'And we do *not* have termites!' and hung up."

■ ■ ■ ■ ■ ■ ■ ■ ■ ■ ■

Fourteen

■

A Worse Idea

Wally crouched between the rake and the lawn mower and tried to see through the narrow crack in the door.

"What's he doing?" Jake asked. "Is he going over to Mrs. Corby's yet?"

"No. He's coming around the side of our house," said Wally. "I think he's going to knock on the back door."

"Oh, man!" breathed Josh. "What if he comes out here? What'll we say?"

"How do you do, what else?" said Wally, wishing for the hundredth time that he hadn't got mixed up in this. The huge termite on top of the white truck out by the curb seemed to have one eye on the Hatfords' toolshed at the back of the yard, and Wally could almost imagine it was watching him through the crack.

Jake climbed over the wheelbarrow and nudged Wally aside so he could see out.

"Oh, boy!" he whispered. "He *is* knocking. And now he's looking all around the yard!"

"Maybe he's inspected the outside of our house for termites and he'll inspect the shed next," said Josh.

"I'm hot!" Peter complained from his perch inside the wheelbarrow. "I can't breathe in this shed!"

"Shhhhh. Don't talk so loud, Peter. Oh, no! He *is* starting back here!" Josh said.

"What are we gonna do?" said Josh. "Suddenly burst out of the toolshed and yell 'Surprise'?"

Wally considered picking up a burlap sack and pulling it over his head.

"Wait," whispered Jake. "Now he's stopped. Now he's looking toward the house next door. Yay! He's going around in front again. I think he's going over to the Corbys'. He *is* going next door! All we need is for him to knock on Mrs. Corby's door while the girls are over there."

This will never work, Wally thought. Things never turned out quite the way Jake planned them. Wally considered going around with a burlap sack over his head for the rest of his life.

"I'm going to melt!" Peter warned.

"Just a few more minutes, Peter, and then he'll be gone," said Jake.

"I'm turning into butter!" Peter wailed.

"There he goes, up on the Corbys' front porch!" said Jake. "Hey! The girls are coming out! They've seen him! They almost bumped into him. Is this perfect, or is this perfect?"

"I'm starting to ooze," said Peter from the wheelbarrow.

Josh took his place at the crack in the door. "Mrs. Corby's talking to him now. She's sending him away, and the girls are staring after him. You just know they'll go home and tell their folks!"

"Did he leave?" asked Wally.

"Yep. He's going back to his truck. And the girls are leaving too," said Josh. "Wait one more minute, Peter, and we'll get out of here."

The boys opened the door of the toolshed at last and stepped out into the fresh air. Their heads were wet with perspiration, and sweat trickled down their backs.

"Saved!" yelled Jake, and they went into the house for some lemonade.

■

Mr. Hatford wore shorts with his postal uniform now. He said that summer was his favorite season, and he loved going door-to-door in his shirtsleeves. When he came in that afternoon, he wanted a glass of lemonade too, and he sat out on the glider, swirling the ice around in his glass.

"Have you guys collected any more money for the hospital?" he asked.

"One more car wash should do it," said Josh. "We told the Malloys we'd hold it over here this Saturday."

"Fair enough," said his dad. "Put a sign at the corner so folks will know to turn this way."

This was the evening Mrs. Hatford came home for dinner, then went back to the hardware store to work until nine o'clock. On warm nights like this, she served her family a cold salad with hard-boiled eggs and corn muffins. Cold salad did not seem like real supper to Wally, however, and his dad must have felt the same way, because after Mr. Hatford had eaten the salad, he got up to get some ice cream.

At that moment there was a knock at the front door, so he went to answer it instead.

"Good evening," Wally heard a man say. "I hope I'm not interrupting your dinner, but we received a call that someone here wanted a termite inspection. I came by earlier but no one was home."

Wally began a slow slide off his chair.

"Termites?" said Mr. Hatford. And then, more loudly, "Ellen? Do we have termites?"

"Termites!" cried Mrs. Hatford, scooting away from the table and heading for the front door. "Who said we have termites?"

Wally's chin had almost disappeared beneath the table, and Jake and Josh sat frozen, eyes unblinking.

"All I know, ma'am, is that I got a call from our

dispatcher asking me to check out this house and the one next door. Lady over there didn't know anything about it."

"Well, for goodness' sake, who could have called?" Mrs. Hatford said. "We're right in the middle of dinner, but you can take a look if you like."

"I'll take him down to the basement, Ellen," Mr. Hatford said. "Josh, make sundaes for the rest of the family, would you?"

Josh got out of his chair and walked to the counter like a robot. He put a scoopful of ice cream and a spoonful of syrup in six bowls and set them on the table, but no one was eating except Peter. When the exterminator came up from the basement at last and pronounced the home termite free, he left, and Mr. Hatford came back to the table.

"Well, that's good news, anyway," Mr. Hatford said, sitting back down. "But who could have called? Does our house look like it has termites?"

"Where were you boys this afternoon when he came by?" asked their mother.

"I thought we weren't supposed to open the door to strangers," Jake answered.

"Yeah!" said Peter. "We were hiding in the toolshed."

Jake and Josh and Wally stared daggers at Peter, who quickly concentrated on his ice cream again. But Mr. and Mrs. Hatford studied each of their sons in turn.

"Hiding? Why?" asked Wally's father.

And Peter, knowing he had goofed up before, tried

to correct the matter. "Because we knew we didn't have termites and didn't want him to come in," he said.

"So why didn't you just call out and tell him to come another time?" asked Mrs. Hatford.

Jake shrugged.

Mr. Hatford raised an eyebrow. "Let me get this straight: an exterminator knocks at our front door and you guys go hide in the toolshed? What did you think he was going to do? Exterminate *you*?"

"We were scared of that big old bug on top of his truck," said Peter, nodding emphatically.

Mr. Hatford leaned back in his chair. "Wally, you're about to slide under the table," he said. "Do you want to tell me what this is all about?"

"Not particularly," said Wally. "Ask Jake."

Mr. Hatford turned to Jake.

"We just thought...well, with the Corbys moving and everything, maybe they should have their house inspected for termites before they rented it. We were just trying to be helpful."

Mrs. Hatford put down her spoon. "Why would it even *occur* to you to do something like that? Who are you concerned might rent that house and find termites?" And then her face relaxed. "Aha! I think I get it!"

"I think I do too," said Mr. Hatford. "Were you boys by chance hoping the Corbys *did* have termites? Or that the Malloys would see the truck outside and change their minds about renting that house?"

The phone rang, and Wally, glad for an excuse to leave the table, quickly jumped up and answered.

"Hello?" he said.

A woman's voice came out so loudly that he had to hold the receiver away from his ear.

"For your information," Mrs. Corby said, "we do *not* have termites." And she hung up.

■ ■ ■ ■ ■ ■ ■ ■ ■ ■ ■ ■

Fifteen

■

After Dark

It helped that the Hatford boys were in the doghouse too, the girls decided. On the way to school the next morning, Peter blurted out that termites were sure causing a lot of trouble these days, then added, "And Mrs. Corby's really mad!"

Caroline and her sisters looked at Wally, Jake, and Josh, and immediately understood.

"Yeah, she called our place too," said Eddie, "and Mom went ballistic that we'd been over to look at the bedrooms."

"Dad went ballistic that we called an exterminator,"

said Jake. "I don't know why Mrs. Corby was so mad about it, though. It's not like we *hurt* anybody, and she could have had a free inspection."

"So where *are* you going to live if your dad takes another job in Buckman?" Josh asked.

"I don't know," said Beth. "Nobody knows anything. And frankly, I'm not going to worry about it. I'm going to concentrate on enjoying the summer."

"Only two more days of school!" Peter sang out. "And *then*...all the strawberries I can eat!"

"What time do you want to start the car wash on Saturday?" Eddie asked the boys. "Why don't we make it early, and maybe we can earn enough to fill all our collection cans."

"Eight o'clock," said Jake.

"I'll make some signs and put them up around the neighborhood," said Josh.

"And I'll do the wheels!" said Peter happily.

Now that the Hatfords and the Malloys were friends again, it *could* have been a cheerful day. The car wash arrangements were settled, the sun was shining, the birds were singing, and the bees and butterflies were out. When the seven kids walked by Mrs. Corby's house, however, where she was reading on her front porch, she snatched up her newspaper and went inside, banging the screen behind her. And *that*, Caroline decided later, should have told her that the day wasn't going to be so perfect after all.

In Caroline's classroom, as other people stood up to read their reports on where they had chosen to be shipwrecked or plane-wrecked, none of them, Caroline decided, was as good as her report was going to be. But she was practicing to be nice now, and after each report, when Miss Applebaum asked for comments, Caroline raised her hand and said that she thought the report was very good. Sometimes she said it was "very, *very* good." The more complimentary she was to other people when they gave their reports, she figured, the nicer they would be to her.

She was careful, however, not to use words like *fantastic* or *stupendous,* because once she said that about someone else's performance, what words could anyone use to describe Caroline's? All the good words would be taken!

The morning went well. Lunch went well. Her mother had put strawberry jelly in her peanut butter sandwich, not grape, which Caroline hated—and the afternoon was okay too, even though a wasp got in the classroom and she imagined she could feel it crawling through her hair during math.

She played on the rope swing with her sisters after school, enjoyed their dinner of shrimp and rice, and was thinking about going outside to swing again, even though it was growing dark.

Just then she heard her father say, "Jean, do you hear that bird? I've been listening to it for the last couple of evenings. A mockingbird, I think. I'm going to get my binoculars."

Caroline finished brushing her teeth and decided she would look for the bird too while she was swinging. But then she heard her father call, "Does anyone know where my binoculars are? I always keep them on the closet shelf, and they're not there."

And Caroline's day began to crumble.

The *binoculars*! Her head reeled. She could almost see herself walking into Mrs. Corby's house with the binoculars in her hand. She remembered going up Mrs. Corby's stairs holding those binoculars. And then, her heart sinking, she remembered setting her dad's binoculars on a windowsill in one of Mrs. Corby's bedrooms.

Caroline felt sick to her stomach.

"Eddie?" her dad was calling. "Have you seen my binoculars? Beth?"

Caroline knew she was next, and before he could call out her name, she slipped out of the bathroom and down the stairs. Out the door she went, and down the hill toward the footbridge.

There was nothing else to be done. She was going to have to knock on Mrs. Corby's door and tell her she had left something in one of the bedrooms. Humiliation, that was what it was. She tried to console herself with the thought that if she ever had to play the part of a humiliated woman, she would know how it felt. The burning cheeks, the pounding heart, the dry throat, the thick tongue...

Caroline took a deep breath as she neared the Corbys' house, and then she saw Mrs. Corby out weeding her flower bed in the twilight.

Luck was with her! Maybe Fate had decided she had

suffered enough! Maybe because she was practicing being nice to people, God had decided to make it easy for her. Creeping up on the porch, she tried the screen door and, just as she expected, it was unlocked.

There was a lamp burning in the living room, but Caroline tiptoed on by and softly, stealthily, like a panther, moved up the stairs. The hallway above was dark and lined with small tables and trunks. Caroline could barely see where she was going and stumbled once as she bumped into a chair.

When she reached the first bedroom, she moved inside, feeling her way along and heading for the windows. Her hands slid over first one windowsill, then another. Nothing. Maybe Mrs. Corby had already found the binoculars and was keeping them for her own!

Back to the hall again, and into the next bedroom. Caroline moved past a dresser, a bed, barely able to see them in the meager light from downstairs. And there, on the windowsill, were her father's binoculars, just where she had left them. She gave a little murmur of thanks as she picked them up and turned around.

And then she screamed. In the dark doorway stood the figure of a man with a shaggy head, holding a club in his hand.

The light came on and an elderly man holding a rolled-up magazine stared at her quizzically.

"Who the dickens are *you*?" he asked.

"Wh...who are *you*?" Caroline responded.

"The owner of this house, for one thing," the man

said, and Caroline remembered that there *was* a *Mr.* Corby. The man had a gray beard that stuck out an inch all around his face. "I happen to live here," he said. "But unless you're a long-lost granddaughter, I can't say the same for you."

"I...I just came over to get something I left the other day," Caroline said, wishing he would move a little to one side so that she could squeeze past him and run downstairs.

"Those wouldn't happen to be binoculars, would they?" Mr. Corby asked.

"Yes," said Caroline.

"You wouldn't have happened to be spying the other day, would you?"

"N—not exactly," said Caroline.

"You didn't happen to come over here with binoculars to spy on the boys next door, did you?" Mr. Corby asked, and Caroline wasn't sure, but it looked as though he might be hiding a smile. Because she was too embarrassed to answer, he said, "Well, you'd better get on home, then. I'd say that between you and those Hatford boys, you've caused enough trouble already." And as Caroline gratefully left the room and hurried down the stairs, he called after her, "And if you brought any termites over here, take them with you."

Caroline bolted from the house just as she heard the back screen door slam and Mrs. Corby call, "Harold, did you hear somebody scream a minute ago?" Caroline ran down the sidewalk and right smack into Wally Hatford.

"I thought I heard somebody scream," Wally said.

"You did," said Caroline, rubbing her forehead where they had collided and hurrying by to get out from under the streetlight.

"What were you doing in the Corbys' house with binoculars?" Wally asked, following her. And then, "I'll bet you were trying to see us in our underwear or something."

Caroline had had just about enough for one day. She wheeled about and faced him. "You're right," she said, "and you know what? Looking at Wally Hatford in his underwear would be about the most boring thing in the universe. We're not going to rent that house and we're not going to be in those bedrooms and we're not going to watch you through binoculars, so relax."

"That's good," said Wally. "Because if I ever got plane-wrecked somewhere, being plane-wrecked with *you* would be about the most boring thing I could think of."

"Good!" said Caroline. "So we agree."

She went down the bank and on across the foot-bridge toward home. But Wally's remark stung. That simply could not be true! She might be unpleasant at times. She might be self-centered, but Caroline Lenore Malloy was *never* boring! And if Wally Hatford didn't believe that, he could just wait till she stood up in front of the class tomorrow and gave her report!

■ ■ ■ ■ ■ ■ ■ ■ ■ ■ ■ ■

Sixteen

■

Turnaround

The last day of school had come, and Wally was ready for it to be over. After he gave his stupid report in that stupid room in front of that stupid class, he wouldn't have to think about school again till September. By that time, either the Malloys would have gone back to Ohio, or they would have moved to another house in Buckman. Either way, the Benson boys would be back, and that was something to look forward to.

Actually, the plane-wreck project was probably the most interesting one the fourth grade had had all year, so maybe it wasn't so stupid after all. Giving a report in front of the class, though, was something else. Wally had already decided that he would go first that day so he could stop worrying about it. But he was a second too late, because Caroline waved her hand in front of the teacher's face, and Caroline got to go first.

She opened her backpack and pulled out a safari hat. She pulled out a compass, a whistle, and a raincoat. Then she put on the hat and walked dramatically to the front of the room, where she propped up a painting she had done of her location in Australia. After that, she read a report that sounded to Wally like paragraphs from a girl's diary:

"Our plane crashed and my knee is so sore I can hardly walk, but the pilot can't walk at all. He's dead," she read to the class.

Then she described the weather in Australia's outback, and the way she had carried rocks from a riverbank to spell out *HELP* on a hillside. And as if that weren't enough, she turned to the blackboard and wrote out a recipe for wombat stew. And then . . . *then* she read in closing:

"After a month in the outback with only kangaroos for company, I decided to take my chances on the open sea, in hopes that rescuers would find me there. Making my way to the shoreline, I made a raft of driftwood, packed up my food, brought all the water I could carry and, using my raincoat for a sail, I set off. I finally arrived at the island of Banaba, where I found Wally Hatford, and together we lived out our lives in peace and harmony."

Smiling smugly, Caroline sat back down.

Everyone began laughing and pointing at Wally. His

neck was on fire, he was sure of it. His cheeks and forehead burned. He didn't wait to be called on. He didn't even raise his hand. He grabbed his report and stomped to the front of the room.

He told how he had been shipwrecked and made it to the island of Banaba in the Pacific. He told what he had done to survive, and then he said, "One day I looked out and saw a girl sailing toward shore on a homemade raft. I could tell by the way she acted that she was crazy, so before she could reach my camp, I packed up and moved to the other side of the island and I never saw her again. The end."

Everyone laughed some more, even Miss Applebaum.

"Well, she said, "I guess we have a difference of opinion here. Caroline, maybe you should have quit while you were ahead." Then she called on another person to give a report, and Wally sank back in his seat, victorious at last. Out the window the sky had never looked so blue, the clouds so white, the sun so bright as on that day when he got even with Caroline Malloy.

■

That afternoon, no one did any work at all. They held a survivor party, and each person got a small compass along with his or her report card. As a treat, Miss Applebaum cracked open a fresh coconut. Everyone had a piece of coconut meat along with a slice of banana and some fresh blueberries, typical survivor foods. Wally and his friends had fun turning around and around and watching the needles on their compasses spin with them.

Finally, when the last bell rang, everyone spilled out onto the steps and sidewalk like ants from an anthill. Peter was already frolicking about on the grass, singing:

> *"School's out! School's out!*
> *Teacher let the monkeys out!*
> *One jumped in, one jumped out,*
> *One jumped in the teacher's mouth!"*

At last! Wally thought. No more reports. No more school. No more Caroline Malloy sitting behind him.

■

By six o'clock that evening, Josh had posted signs all over the neighborhood reading, FOUR-DOLLAR CAR WASH, INSIDE AND OUT, and giving the address. And by eight o'clock the next morning, there were already three cars lined up, ready to pull into the Hatfords' driveway.

"Boys!" Mrs. Hatford said. "I've left sandwiches and lemonade in the fridge for all of you, and there are more clean rags on the porch if you need them. Be careful, now. Josh, I want you personally to keep an eye on Peter when cars pull in and out."

"I will," Josh promised.

She left for her job at the hardware store, and Mr. Hatford came downstairs in his postal uniform. "Be sure to clean the inside of each windshield and wipe off the dashboard," he said, coffee cup in hand. Then he left for the post office, and the first car in line came up the drive.

The girls had arrived even before the boys came outside, and now they all pitched in. The day couldn't have been better—breezy, warm, and dry, and everyone cheered each time a truly dirty car pulled in with mud caked on the spokes of the hubcaps, because these were the most fun to wash. Wally liked turning a filthy car into a spanking-clean one.

The kids took turns walking down to the corner and pointing to the car wash sign as people drove by, motioning them back to the Hatfords'. When Mrs. Corby next door came outside, hands on her hips, to see what those Hatford boys and Malloy girls were up to now, they offered to wash her car for free, and that took the scowl off her face in a hurry.

The money was piling up in a shoe box inside the front door, and Josh had already figured that after they divided it seven ways, they each would have earned the twenty dollars needed to be in the parade. Strawberry festival, here they came!

At about three that afternoon, when there was a lull in business and not a car in sight, Wally was picking up some wet cloths on the driveway beside Beth and Eddie when suddenly, *plop!* Out of nowhere, it seemed, there was an explosion between him and Eddie, and they were both showered with water. Wally had barely let out a yelp when there was a second explosion right at Caroline's feet. She gasped and coughed, water dripping from her ears and nose, and when they all looked toward the house, they saw Jake and Josh with the hose and a pile of balloons filled with water.

The war was on—first, to see who could get control of the hose, and second, to reach the supply of water balloons the twins had filled the night before. Howls and cries of revenge filled the air as the girls ran this way, the boys ran that way, and the hose changed hands a dozen times as everyone got royally soaked.

It was hard to see which side Peter was on, because first he helped the girls out, then his brothers.

"Hey, Peter, whose friend are you, anyway?" Josh laughed as Peter inadvertently turned the hose on Wally.

And just as Wally wrested the hose from Peter's hands, he saw, coming up the driveway, the washing machine, the dryer, and three more boys, each half the size of a refrigerator. They were big boys, tough-looking boys, and they had come to close down the car wash, it said so right on their faces.

"Wally! Peter! Up here!" Jake yelled out the warning, and all the Malloys and Hatfords gathered on the porch. The assembly line had never worked more efficiently. Balloons were filled, tied, and thrown at the enemy, and between throws, the hose soaked each intruder in turn.

Then the intruders got possession of the hose, and water went flying in every direction. It took only minutes before a dozen kids looked as though they had just climbed out of the river, their clothes clinging to their bodies like plastic wrap.

Back and forth the hose went, from one side to the other. The five large boys who had come up the drive took over the Hatfords' porch now, turning the hose on its rightful owners. Out of the corner of his eye, Wally saw Josh and Jake coming around the house with an emergency supply of water balloons.

Wally's heart was in his mouth. This would only end badly, he was sure. Even if they won the battle, he and Peter would have to face those bullies by themselves in September when Jake and Josh went off to seventh grade. Those tough appliances would be lying in wait, and someday, sometime, they would probably get Wally and Peter alone and stick their heads down a toilet. Every time a water balloon hit one of the intruders and exploded, Wally could almost feel another thwack on his back or a punch in the belly when the bullies decided to go for him.

At that moment a car turned into the Hatfords' driveway and a woman tentatively stuck her head out the window. "Is the car wash still doing business?" she asked.

The Malloys looked at the Hatfords and the Hatfords looked at the bullies, who turned the hose sideways on the bushes. In the sudden lull, Eddie sneaked over and turned off the outside faucet. The hose went dry.

"Sure," Josh called to the woman. He looked at his soaked companions. Then he looked at the boy with the hose. "Well," he said, "it doesn't look like you guys could get any wetter. We've already made enough money to be in the parade. Do you want to do the next cars?"

The washing machine, the dryer, and the three refrigerators looked at each other. They looked as if they would like to drag the Hatfords down the hill to the river and throw them in.

"You can use our hose and our rags," added Wally helpfully.

"Business or war. You have to choose one or the other," said Jake.

The washing machine pondered it a little more.

"Well, I guess we can do the car," he said finally. Eddie turned the water back on, and for a moment the boy seemed to be debating whether to use it on the car or on Jake. But at last he nodded toward his friends and they began to wash the car.

The Hatfords and Malloys watched from the sidelines, and when another car pulled in, the intruders motioned where it should park and turned the hose on it.

Wally took a deep breath and sat down on the porch steps with his brothers, peace restored to the kingdom at last.

Seventeen

■

Strawberry Shortcake

It was the first week of summer vacation, and time to return the collection cans to the bank in preparation for Saturday's festival. As the kids lined up, they were given cards to fill out stating whether they would prefer all the strawberry treats they could eat or a place in the parade, and just where in the parade they would most like to be.

All I have ever wanted in this life, in the whole world, is to ride on the float with the Strawberry Queen of Buckman, Caroline wrote on her card.

This was not quite true, of course, because what Caroline wanted most in the world was to be an actress on Broadway. In fact, it wasn't the least little bit true because she hadn't even heard of the Strawberry Festival, the parade, or the queen until they'd moved to West Virginia.

But with Eddie involved in summer baseball and Beth helping out at the library and the Hatford boys busily planning for the Bensons' return, Caroline felt she would shrink up and die if she was not allowed to ride beside the Strawberry Queen on Saturday and wave delicately to the crowd. She might shrivel up anyway, she thought, for the breeze that had made the car wash day so delightful seemed to have deserted them entirely, and the air grew warmer still. Those who had hoped it would not rain on their parade now almost began to hope that it would, just to cool things off.

When Caroline got a last-minute call from a woman who wanted her to take over at a birthday party because the clown she had hired got sick, Caroline realized that her notice was still up on the bulletin board.

"Oh, Mother, no!" she cried when Mrs. Malloy gave her the message. She did *not* want to perform for any more rude, thankless children. She did *not* want to be pushed into an imaginary oven or try to be heard onstage with a lawn mower going next door.

"Caroline, you said you were available for parties, and until that notice comes down, that's your job," her mother said. "The woman who called is a friend of one of the professors at the college, and she seemed desperate to find some entertainment for the party."

So Caroline called the woman back to find out what

fairy tale she wanted. This time the request was for "Goldilocks and the Three Bears," and the guests at the party would be four-year-olds. Caroline managed to find a cap with bear ears on it, and furry mittens for paws. And though the four-year-olds romped about on the floor and tried to take her cap off, they were more attentive than the six-year-olds had been. If Caroline had been wearing a tail, she would have wagged it when she was through, she was so happy the performance went well.

■

Thursday, the three Malloy girls received postcards in the mail giving them the name and number of the float each of them would be on.

"Hey! I get to ride with the women's basketball team from the college!" Eddie yelped delightedly. "All *right*!"

Beth got to be a bookworm on the library's float.

Caroline was so eager to read her card that she fumbled and dropped it, but then she saw the number two, and beside it the treasured words *Strawberry Queen Float*. She shrieked with happiness.

Eddie took the card away from her to be sure she wasn't faking it. "Look what else it says, Caroline," she said, pointing to a note at the bottom: *Please wear a bathing suit.*

"What?" cried Caroline. She was going to be a bathing beauty as well?

"Don't wear a bikini, Caroline," Eddie said, glancing at her sister's midsection. "*Please* don't wear a bikini."

"This," said Caroline dramatically, "is beyond my wildest dreams."

"Well, if you're going to be standing on a float wearing a bathing suit, we'd better buy you a new one," Mrs. Malloy said. "The yellow suit you wore last summer was a little too snug even then."

So off they went, and Caroline and her mother returned an hour later with a one-piece suit—a red one with pink polka dots and a narrow pink ruffle around the neckline.

"Isn't it beautiful?" Caroline gushed. "I chose it myself."

"You look like a cupcake," Beth muttered.

"At least it's a *strawberry* cupcake!" Caroline retorted.

"Strawberry shortcake, that's you," said Eddie.

■

The day of the parade arrived at last, and Caroline was so excited she could barely contain herself. Her mother had also bought her a wide-brimmed hat so that she wouldn't get sunburned, and a pair of sunglasses as well.

Eddie was wearing a T-shirt, shorts, and a baseball cap, and Beth had been told that all the bookworms on her float would be given headdresses to wear, with feelers and big goggle eyes.

Unfortunately, the day was not just warm, it was hot—as hot as anyone could remember it being in Buckman in June. When Caroline looked out the window that morning, not a leaf stirred. Not a blade of

129

grass moved. Everything seemed to sizzle under the gaze of the silent sun.

All the kids who were to be part of the parade were to meet at the Buckman High School parking lot, where the floats were lining up. Mr. and Mrs. Malloy dropped off their three daughters, then drove back downtown to park and find a shady spot where they could watch the action.

"See you!" Eddie said to the others as she set off to find her float.

"Have fun!" Beth said to Caroline as she headed for hers.

Caroline, in her new bathing suit, walked toward the front of the lineup, looking for float number two, and there it was, a beautiful float decorated with artificial strawberries and roses. The Strawberry Queen herself, a redheaded college girl wearing a pink puffy dress and a crown of strawberries, stood in the shade of a tree off to one side, where her mother fanned her.

Her throne, a red padded chair, had a sheet stretched over the top of it temporarily as a canopy to keep the seat cool until the parade began.

To Caroline's disappointment, two younger girls from Buckman Elementary also showed up in bathing suits, each of them carrying a card that read *float number two*.

Oh, well, thought Caroline, looking them over. She herself was probably the prettiest of the three, and at least her bathing suit was the color of strawberries, not green or purple like the two younger girls'.

But queens, she knew, were supposed to be generous. They were supposed to be nice to everybody whether they felt like it or not, so she smiled at the girls and said wasn't it hot and wasn't the Strawberry Queen beautiful and weren't they all lucky to get to be on the float along with her?

But all the while, Caroline's eyes were on the Strawberry Queen. Maybe Caroline would stand to the right of her in her bathing suit and help adjust her crown if it slipped. Maybe Caroline would stand to the left of her and refill the little basket of strawberry candies the queen was supposed to toss to the crowd. Or perhaps Caroline, in her pink and red polka-dot bathing suit, would sit at the feet of the Strawberry Queen to keep her skirt from blowing in the breeze. If there was a breeze.

There was not even the slightest hint of a breeze. Already Caroline could feel a trickle of sweat roll down her back between her shoulder blades.

A gray-haired woman in red shorts with an official badge pinned to her T-shirt came hurrying up.

"Ah! My helpers have arrived!" she said, smiling at Caroline and the two younger girls. "The parade is about to start, so we're going to get you up on the float. As soon as the Strawberry Queen gets on and settled, we'll go." She hustled them over to the movable wooden steps leading to the float.

The girls grinned excitedly at each other and followed the parade official up the steps and onto the flatbed truck carrying the queen's chair, a bower of strawberries and roses overhead.

Caroline started toward the chair, but the parade official clasped her arm and said, "Follow me."

Caroline's heart fell as they went to the back of the float instead. There, she saw three giant-size velveteen strawberries.

The official smiled at the smallest girl. "You first," she said, and held open a slit in the back of one of the strawberries.

In dismay, Caroline watched as the youngest girl climbed uncertainly into the huge strawberry.

"Stick your head out the hole in the top," the woman instructed her, "and your arms out the holes on either side."

A small blond head popped up where the stem of the strawberry would be, followed by two small arms through the holes on either side.

"Perfect!" said the official. "Now, remember to smile and wave at the crowd. Next!"

As she watched the second girl climb into the next strawberry, Caroline could not believe this was happening. This was it? This was what Caroline Lenore Malloy had waited for all this time? She had washed all those cars and endured that terrible birthday party just so she could be a stupid strawberry, sweltering up here on a ninety-degree day?

When her turn came, she stepped numbly into the hot velveteen strawberry. She thrust her head through the hole at the top, where the scratchy green leaves chafed her neck. The right arm through the right hole, left arm through the left, and there she was, like a pilgrim put in the stocks. She turned her head to the left and the leaves scratched her cheek. She turned to the right and the leaves scratched her ear.

Help! thought Caroline as the parade official disappeared, the band began to play, and slowly, with a fire engine in front, the parade began moving toward Main Street.

■ ■ ■ ■ ■ ■ ■ ■ ■ ■ ■

Eighteen

■

Queen for a Day

When Wally got his card in the mail, it said simply, STATION NUMBER 3. It did not give the name of a float. Jake's card said he was going to ride on the fire truck with a dozen other guys, and Josh's card said he got to ride in the car with the mayor and two more boys from his class. But Wally had no idea where he would be in the parade.

"I'll be watching for you guys," Mrs. Hatford said that morning. She had taken the day off work to stay with Peter at the festival. "All the folks at the hardware store will be waving to you."

Peter, clutching his tickets for treats, was eager to get going and taste those strawberries, and Mr. Hatford said he would do his mail deliveries in the business district first so that he could see the parade too.

"Jump in my car and I'll drop you off at the high school," he told the older boys, and Wally and the twins climbed into the backseat.

There weren't as many kids at the school as Wally had thought. Evidently a lot had collected some money and then stopped. Everyone who had turned in any money at all got a coupon for strawberry shortcake, but perhaps only thirty or so had earned the right to be in the parade.

"Have a good time!" Mr. Hatford said as they piled out of the car.

"Bye!" said Josh excitedly as he went over to shake hands with the mayor.

"See ya!" said Jake as he headed for the fire truck, which was first in the lineup.

Wally stood still and looked around him. If the fire truck was number one, and the Strawberry Queen float was number two, then number three had to be . . . Wally looked around some more. There *was* no number three. Number four followed number two, and that was the Women's Garden Club float.

Wally decided that if *that* was station number three, he would turn around and go home. He would not wear a petunia costume and wave to the crowd. He would not toss daisies to people or dress up like a tulip.

Just as he turned to go back down the line again, three policemen rode up on horseback and took their places behind the queen's float.

"You looking for station number three?" one of them asked.

Wally's heart sank. He knew it! He would be the parade pooper scooper. His job would be to walk behind the horses and shovel up manure. Slowly he nodded his head.

One of the policemen slid off his horse and said, "Over here. You get to ride the bay."

Wally stared. *"What?"* he said.

"Not afraid, are you?" The officer smiled. "She's really a good old horse, and you've got Mac and Sam here to keep an eye on things."

Wally couldn't believe it. Nothing good ever seemed to happen to him, but this was for real.

The policeman showed him how to put one foot in the stirrup and swing his other leg over the back of the horse. And there he was! Wally Hatford! Sitting high on a horse between two officers.

He didn't mind that the saddle leather was hot beneath him. He didn't care that the horse's flanks were warm. He wasn't even scared when the bay snorted and shook her mane. Wally held the reins in his hand like a longtime cowboy. He had never felt better in his life.

He looked around at the crowd on his left. He looked around at the crowd on his right. Then he looked straight ahead and almost fell off the horse, because he thought he saw a giant strawberry wave at him. *Three* humongous strawberries, as a matter of fact. He was sure he saw them move.

Well, their arms, maybe. Yes, they *did* have arms. And then he saw that each strawberry had a head right where the stem should be. And then . . . *then* . . . he saw that one of the heads belonged to none other than Caroline Lenore Malloy.

Wally could only stare in astonishment as the parade began to move. He couldn't tell if the streaks on Caroline's cheeks were tears or sweat, but she definitely did not look happy. Wanly, Caroline smiled to the left and then to the right. Feebly she waved her left hand, then her right.

Clang! Clang! went the bell on the fire truck. *Thumpa thumpa thumpa* went a drum somewhere behind him. *Clickity clackity* went the horses' hooves on the pavement as Wally and the two policemen trotted along behind the queen's float. Wally could not see the queen herself, but he could see candy flying out to the left, then to the right, and the crowds reaching out to catch it.

They went past the hospital, where patients in wheelchairs had been brought out in front to watch. Past the courthouse, where Wally's dad whistled and waved, his eyes wide with surprise as Wally rode by. Past the theater and the drugstore, on past Ethel's Bakery and Oldakers' Bookstore.

Booths up and down Main Street sold strawberry ice

cream, strawberry shortcake, and strawberry pancakes dusted with powdered sugar.

"Hey, look at Wally!" came a cry from Peter, who grabbed his mother's arm and pointed. His mouth was smeared red with fresh strawberries.

"For heaven's sake!" cried Mrs. Hatford. "Why, it's Wally on a horse!"

Wally beamed. This was ten times better than riding on the fire truck. Twenty times better than riding with the mayor. Thirty times better than marching behind the band.

They passed the hardware store and the department store, the beauty parlor and the college. When they got to Buckman Elementary, where the parade was to turn around and go back, Wally saw people sitting along the wall, up on the steps, even on top of the jungle gym.

Suddenly, the fire engine stopped. The queen's float stopped. Little by little the whole parade stopped moving, but the band played on.

Wally saw two firemen jump down from the truck up ahead and come running back to the queen's float. There was a great deal of movement and confusion, and the two officers on either side of Wally quickly rode up to see what was going on, motioning Wally to come along.

"What's the trouble?" one of the officers called.

"The queen's fainted. Heat exhaustion, I imagine," the first fireman answered. "I've put in a call for an ambulance."

Wally nosed his horse up to the front of float number two, and there was the strawberry queen lying in a heap at the foot of her throne.

"We're going to carry her over there into the shade," the second fireman said. "Joe will stay with her until the ambulance comes."

"We need to get this parade moving again," said the policeman next to Wally. "Can't have all these folks just standing out under the sun."

At that moment Caroline Malloy burst out of her velveteen strawberry at the back of the float and came running around to the front. "*I'll* do it! *I'll* do it!" she called. "I'll sit on the throne and throw out candy to the crowd."

The policemen and firemen looked at the girl in the bright red bathing suit with the large pink polka dots. One of the firemen smiled.

"Well, sweetheart, I guess you're as close to a strawberry as we're going to get, so you climb up there with your basket and we'll get started."

An ambulance came down a side street, weaving in and out of the crowd, but the parade was on its way, first the fire truck, then the queen's float, then Wally and the policemen. Wally couldn't see Caroline sitting on the throne up ahead, but he could see candy whizzing to the left, candy whizzing to the right, and as they turned around in the school parking lot to head back up Main Street again, he caught a glimpse of Caroline, the crown of strawberries on her head, throwing candy to the crowd with one hand and kisses with the other, as though she had lived in a palace all her life and knew exactly what to do.

The firemen were smiling. The policemen were smiling. Wally was smiling too. Was this wild or was this nuts? Or did it really matter? School was out, summer had begun, he was on horseback, and if Caroline was queen for a day, so what?

Nineteen

■

Letter to Georgia

Dear Benson Brothers:

I thought you might like to know what you're missing up here in Buckman, so I am enclosing a picture of me on the Strawberry Queen float in the Strawberry Festival Parade last Saturday. The newspaper article will tell you the story of how I got to be queen. If you look closely, you will see Wally on a horse behind the queen's float. Jake was riding on the fire engine and Josh rode with the mayor. Now aren't you sorry you moved to Georgia?

Beth and Eddie and I are enjoying a delightful summer in your house, and I don't know where we'll move if we stay here in Buckman. I just want you to know that when you come back here and take over your house, you will definitely know we're around. You will definitely know that the Malloy girls can shake things up a little, and that we can do almost anything if we put our minds to it.

Sincerely,
Caroline Lenore Malloy

P.S. The bathing suit is brand-new.

About the Author

There really is an annual strawberry festival in the town of Buckhannon, West Virginia, which serves as the model for Buckman in this book. Maybe the festival is not quite like this one, but it's still a big deal. Phyllis Reynolds Naylor chose this town for her boys-versus-girls books because that is where her husband grew up, and she loves going back to visit.

There are now ten books in the series—*The Boys Start the War, The Girls Get Even, Boys Against Girls, The Girls' Revenge, A Traitor Among the Boys, A Spy Among the Girls, The Boys Return, The Girls Take Over, Boys in Control,* and *Girls Rule!*

Phyllis Reynolds Naylor is the author of more than a hundred books, including the Newbery Award–winning *Shiloh* and the other two books in the Shiloh trilogy, *Shiloh Season* and *Saving Shiloh.* She and her husband live in Bethesda, Maryland. They are the parents of two grown sons and have three grandchildren, Sophia, Tressa, and Garrett Riley.

■ ■ ■ ■ ■ ■ ■ ■ ■ ■ ■

Read all about the Hatford boys and the Malloy girls.

The Boys Start the War

Just when the Hatford brothers are expecting three boys to move into the house across the river, where their best friends used to live, the Malloy girls arrive instead. Wally and his brothers decide to make Caroline and her sisters so miserable that they'll want to go back to Ohio, but they haven't counted on the ingenuity of the girls. From dead fish to dead bodies, floating cakes to floating heads, the pranks continue—first by the boys, then by the girls—until someone is taken prisoner!

The Girls Get Even

Still smarting from the boys' latest trick, the girls are determined to get even. Caroline is thrilled to play the part of Goblin Queen in the school play, especially since Wally Hatford has to be her footman. The boys, however, have a creepy plan for Halloween night. They're certain the girls will walk right into their trap. Little do the boys know what the Malloy sisters have in store.

Boys Against Girls

Abaguchie mania! Caroline Malloy shivers happily when her on-again, off-again enemy Wally Hatford tells her that the remains of a strange animal known as the abaguchie have been spotted in their area. Wally swears Caroline to secrecy and warns her not to search by herself. But Caroline will do anything to find the secret of the bones.

The Girls' Revenge

Christmas is coming, but Caroline Malloy and Wally Hatford aren't singing carols around the tree. Instead, these sworn enemies must interview each other for the dreaded December class project. Caroline, as usual, has a trick up her sleeve that's sure to shock Wally. In the meantime, Wally and his brothers find a way to spy on the Malloy girls at home. The girls vow to get revenge on those sneaky Hatfords with a trap the boys won't soon forget.

A Traitor Among the Boys

The Hatford boys make a New Year's resolution to treat the Malloy girls like sisters. But who says you can't play tricks on sisters? The girls will need to stay one step ahead of the boys and are willing to pay big-time for advance information. Homemade cookies should be all it takes to make a traitor spill the beans. In the meantime, Caroline is delighted with her role in the town play. Don't ask how Beth, Josh, and Wally get roped into it—just wait until showtime, when Caroline pulls her wildest stunt yet!

A Spy Among the Girls

Valentine's Day is coming up, and love is in the air for Beth Malloy and Josh Hatford. When they're spotted holding hands, Josh tells his teasing brothers that he's simply spying on the girls to see what they're plotting next. At the same time, Caroline Malloy, the family actress, decides she must know what it's like to fall in love. Poor Wally Hatford is in for it when she chooses him as the object of her affection!

The Boys Return

It's spring break, and the only assignment Wally Hatford and Caroline Malloy have is to do something they've never done before. Wally's sure that will be a cinch, because the mighty Benson brothers are coming. It will be nonstop action all the way. For starters, the nine Benson and Hatford boys plan to scare the three Malloy sisters silly by convincing them that their house is haunted. Meanwhile, everyone in town has heard that there's a hungry cougar on the prowl. When the kids decide to take a break from their tricks and join forces to catch the cougar, guess who gets stuck with the scariest job?

The Girls Take Over

The Hatford boys and the Malloy girls are ready to outdo each other again. Eddie is the first girl ever to try out for the school baseball team. Now she and Jake are vying for the same position, while Caroline and Wally compete to become class spelling champ. As if that's not enough, the kids decide to race bottles down the rising Buckman River to see whose will travel farthest by the end of the month. Of course, neither team trusts the other, and when the girls go down to the river to capture the boys' bottles, well...it looks as if those Malloy girls may be in over their heads this time!

Boys in Control

Wally Hatford always seems to get a raw deal. The rest of the family goes to the ball game, and he has to stay home to watch over a yard sale. Caroline Malloy writes a silly play for a school project, and he gets roped into costarring in it with her! Things are looking down, especially when the Malloy girls stumble across an embarrassing item from the boys' past. But Wally finally gets his chance to turn the tables on the girls' scheme and prove who's really in control. Boys rule!